SIBONISO

A ZULU PRINCE

WALTER HES

Siboniso: A Zulu Prince
© Walter Hes 2025

A catalogue record for this book is available from the National Library of Australia

ISBN: 978-0-6459340-2-1 (paperback)
ISBN: 978-0-6459340-3-8 (eBook)

Cover designed by Ocean Reeve Publishing
Typesetting by Lankshear Design
Printed by Ingram Spark Lightning Source

Author's Note

Siboniso is a prince of my imagination. My family and I lived in South Africa for eleven years during the 'apartheid' era. As for many freedom-loving people, Mandela's leadership gave us hope, not only for South Africa but for the whole continent.

After Mandela was gone, I wished somebody like Siboniso would emerge, inspiring all people in Africa in the footsteps of Mandela. Loosely based around historic events, the story will take you into the future with hope for cooperation in achieving African unity.

Contents

About the author

Walter grew up in the Netherlands in a loving but financially constrained family of eight children during and after the Second World War. ADHD was not recognised at the time, but in hindsight, it is clear he was—and still is—affected by it. Combined with dyslexia, this made school difficult. By 14, he was working in construction while attending trade school for carpentry.

His military service took him to Dutch New Guinea (now Irian Jaya) as a Navy medical assistant, an experience that broadened his worldview. After a brief construction stint in Malta, he knew he wouldn't settle in his home country. He spent nine years in South Africa, five in Brazil, and eventually settled in Australia with his wife and two daughters. He continually upskilled, earning a degree in Occupational Health and Safety in his fifties and working as a Safety Officer and Manager until retirement.

Though stories had always been in his mind, he never considered writing until a near-fatal accident and two hip replacements left him bedridden for months. Watching the news, he became increasingly concerned about global issues and felt compelled to act.

This turning point inspired him to write stories about people fighting for change, striving for a fairer and more sustainable world.

Prologue

The information on Africa has been mainly sourced from the African Studies Centre, 'At Penn'.

AFRICA

Africa's climate is mainly tropical. About a third of the area consists of deserts.

Africa has fifty-four states and a population of 1.4 billion people. By estimation, in 2045, that figure will be 2.3 billion. Around half of the African people follow Islam and the other half a Christian religion. Both religions have incorporated many indigenous beliefs. Most states in Africa are republics headed by presidents. Africa is the poorest and least developed continent in the world, even though the wealthiest and most developed countries have become more prosperous by corrupting African governments and exploiting their people.

THE ZULU TRIBE

The lineage of the Zulu tribe goes back approximately 700 years along the East Coast of Africa. From 1785, under King Shaka, son of King Senzangakhona and Queen Nandi, the Zulu Kingdom in South Africa achieved great significance and became a very proud nation. The Zulu kingdom covered an area from the Pongola River in the north to the Tugela River in the south. The KwaZulu state was an independent kingdom until 1879, later semi-independent under the rule of the South African government. The British invaded the Zulu Kingdom to gain control of their riches and to have a source of cheap labour for the gold mines. The Zulu warriors met them with fierce resistance, winning several battles before the British defeated them at the Battle of Ulundi in 1879, only because they had machine guns that killed around five hundred and wounded more than a thousand.

Zulu babies are often named before they are born. When they are born, a ceremony called '*Imbeleko*' [the introduction of a new baby to their ancestors and the tribe.] A family elder will present the name to the ancestors while they slaughter a goat as a sacrifice. Names signify the family's expectations; for instance, Siboniso means leader or guide.

A few words often used in the Zulu languages are as follows. As a greeting:

"*Sawubonal* [I see you; you are significant to me]."

Responded by:

"*Shiboka* [I am here for you]."

The often-used word, '*Ubunto*', used in isiZulu and isiXhosa, is more an expression of togetherness, meaning, I am because you are; we share compassion and humanity.

Chapter One

Siboniso was dreamily looking out over the beautiful hills surrounding the town of Nongoma, in KwaZulu-Natal. He was only six and the first son of King Goodwill, born before his father married any of his six wives. All that is known is that his mother died while giving birth and so the royal household cared for the baby.

The King fathered twenty-eight children and therefore Siboniso grew up surrounded by family and was never lonely. Still, he mostly stayed at the palace of the King's great-wife, Mantfombi Dlamini.

From the age of five, one of Siboniso's duties was watching his father's herd of goats with the older boys in the family, including the sons of his favourite uncle, Mangosuthu Buthelezi.

Siboniso often spent hours daydreaming instead of watching the goats; his cousins did not mind as he was the youngest of them and the King's son. There were enough boys to herd the goats while the grownups watched over the cows. That Siboniso was daydreaming did not mean he was lazy for, when asked, he would jump up and do his bit.

He thought about everything he had to remember, for instance, his three names: Siboniso, Londisizwe, and Blekizizwe. Why was one not enough?

Then, he had to learn several different languages, as was

the custom in the Zulu tribe, not just because he was a part of the royal family. IsiZulu was the most used, but isiXhosa was close. To get around, you also had to learn the Afrikaans language that the local farmers spoke and all the people who worked for the national government ... now that language was a real tongue breaker.

As if that was not enough, the shopkeepers spoke English, which the children of the King also had to learn at the mission school, in addition to Afrikaans and Swahili. They said that you could make yourself understood throughout Africa with those languages, not that these young kids had any idea how large the continent was.

The other boys liked to tease him by speaking languages different from the one used in the royal household. Unintentionally, by doing so, they gave the King's son, whom they called Sib, much practice.

Siboniso was an intelligent boy. He was eager to learn everything about the history of the Zulu Kingdom, and he became fluent in the five languages. This was to prove an asset for the rest of his life.

Advisors to the Zulu king are called indunas. They often act as a bridge between the people and the king. When Siboniso was a bit older, the King ordered his senior induna, to take several princes to the local court to observe how Zulu justice works. His father often met with the indunas to discuss regulations or administrative matters. Siboniso had attended these discussions before but found them boring. However, today he knew that it was going to be exciting.

The King did not always participate in the judicial process, but this day, he was, and as king, he had the final say. The chiefs from the area came together to present criminal cases to the court. The princes were only allowed to stay for a minor case before returning to the King's palace for a discussion.

On this day, this particular case presented to the court was that the local headman had caught a man stealing a ladder from his shed. The accused tried to explain that he needed a ladder to repair his roof and planned to return it. The chiefs listened to what each party had to say before their spokesperson said to the accused: "This is the second time you are before us, is it not?"

The man fell to his knees and cried out: "No, that wasn't me, not me!" However, the court's records did indeed identify that the man had been in the court before on a stealing charge.

"Get up," the judge said, "and explain why you continue to steal. We told you the last time that if you offended again, you would have to pay for your crime."

The accused told the chiefs he struggled to look after his sick wife and their kids. He first appeared before the court when he stole a pumpkin, as they had nothing to eat. This time, he asked the local headman to borrow his ladder, but the man chased him away. So, when nobody was looking, he took the ladder to fix the roof, intending to return it.

The judge asked his advisors what their findings were. They told him that they had interviewed the poor man's neighbours. He had told the truth. After consulting with the chiefs, the King called the offender and the accuser to stand before him.

"Both of you have been at fault," he said. "Do not take what is not yours; we do not steal in our community and do not refuse help when needed."

He looked at the poor man and said, "You have to apologise for your crime and work six hours weekly for the headman. You will only get paid for three hours."

Then he looked at the headman. "You will assist the thief in fixing his roof and give him work for six hours a week but only pay him for three hours."

His final decree was: "Both of you are ordered back here in one month."

Wow, that was interesting. When the boys returned to the King's rondavel, the King asked if they agreed with the verdict.

One of the boys replied that he would have imposed a much higher penalty, but Sib disagreed. He commented that the judgement upheld Zulu standards and values. Both parties must prove they can live peacefully without stealing or refusing help. The King was pleased and impressed with Siboniso's understanding at such an early age.

His father was a good and fair king from a lengthy line of royalty before him. He had been brought up in the tradition of his great-great-grandfather, the Zulu king Shaka. King Goodwill Zwelithini was well respected.

Delegations from the South African government and big mining companies often consulted with the King, mainly about training a labour force for the gold mines.

There was one thing that Siboniso had trouble with and, for a long time, could not understand. He had become aware that it seemed that if you had white skin, you were automatically the boss.

Yes, Siboniso thought, *one must respect and listen to parents, elders, and teachers, but why also to any white person, even the stupid ones?* It did not make sense.

However, he and all his friends had to learn this behaviour, sometimes the hard way; it was never easy. In South Africa, where he lived, it was called 'apartheid', and it was law.

The law described how the different races should live separately, with whites enjoying the most rights and blacks the least. He did not know it then, but Sib would have to wait until his twenties to experience an apartheid-free society.

At school, he learned about the history of the great Zulu nation, its fierce warriors, and the battles they fought. Sib, proud to be related to King Shaka, was eager to know everything about the great king.

When Sib and his friends played their war games, it was difficult to find boys that would play the rednecks, the English invaders. So, they took turns. In their games, the English never won; the spears won it from the guns every time! But they knew that the redneck's guns had killed thousands of their ancestors. In their hearts, they would always be wary of the white man.

———— ✦ ————

One of the things Sib learned from his mates was that a Zulu man never takes orders from a woman. When he tried to put that into practice at home, Queen Mantfombi—he called her '*Umama*' which means 'mother' in the Zulu language—taught him a painful lesson.

It all came about one day, when he refused to do garden duties because: "Zulu men don't have to obey a woman."

His mother, standing in the kitchen of their royal homestead, was supervising the preparations for the evening meal, at the time. She turned to him with her hands on her hips and in an indignant tone, she said: "Is that so, Siboniso, son? It might be true for your father, the King, but not for you, and never in my home! You are not contributing to our family dinner! Go to your room without food. See you in the morning."

Chapter Two

ANOTHER DAY THAT SIBONISO would never forget was when he landed in the hospital.

This happened after a pain in his underbelly had been bothering him throughout a particular night. Later that morning, the pain became unbearable when playing with his friends, and he went home.

His *umama* tried to soothe the discomfort by applying a traditional mixture of herbs to his belly. She also used the same spices to make tea. When it made him vomit and his temperature shot up, she knew they needed help. She sent a message to his father but did not wait and ordered the King's chauffeur to take her son, accompanied by one of his uncles, straight to the white man's hospital.

Being the son of the Zulu king, they admitted him immediately. Siboniso could only remember a little of the trip and the first day. Soon after arriving there, they gave him an injection. He slept until the following morning and discovered that his tummy was hurting less and that he felt a bit better.

After another injection and more sleep, he improved more and became curious about his surroundings. He found himself in a freshly cleaned bed, sharing a ward with seven other black people of all ages. The head nurse was white, but the other nurses were all black.

Everybody was friendly, but nobody gave him food, even though he was hungry. When the kitchen staff brought food for the patients, he was only allowed a drink. One of the Zulu nurses sat down with him. She explained that the antibiotics were healing the inflammation in his belly. He was a lucky boy and did not need an operation to remove his appendix. If the doctor agreed, he would be allowed to eat when his temperature returned to normal.

The next day, the fever was gone, and he was hungrier than ever. He did not have to wait long for the doctor to check him out. The friendly doctor said, winking: "This boy looks very hungry to me. Quickly, give him some food; he might faint!"

A tray with breakfast appeared soon after. Sib ate all of it and asked for more. One of the nurses returned with a cooking pot with left-over *mieliepap* (made from maize) to clean out, but that was it.

The head nurse and the doctor spoke Afrikaans to each other and the nurses. Sib could only pick up a few words, and more when they switched to English. The nurses in this segregated part of the hospital spoke the local languages among themselves and to the patients; there was not much Sib missed.

One day later, the King's driver and one of his uncles came to pick him up from the hospital. On the return journey, he was fascinated by what he saw in the big city.

There were high-rise buildings where people lived on top of each other; towers called churches, headed by a small cross; and many shops in busy streets full of hooting cars and pedestrians. It was an unforgettable experience for a young Zulu boy out of the country.

Back at home, Siboniso heard that his father had been cross with *Umama* for ordering the chauffeur. He declared that he had wanted her first to consult the Sangoma—the local medicine man—before going to the white man's hospital.

The Queen had responded by telling him she knew it was critical when the herbs did not help.

"I was responsible," she stated. "I only wanted the best for your son."

In Zulu culture, it is very unusual for a wife to speak this way to her husband, even more so when her husband is the King. To Siboniso's relief, the King's anger did not last, as he called Sib to him and told him to thank his mother for getting him to the hospital quickly.

— ✦ —

When Siboniso was born, he was welcomed into the royal family, even though his father, Goodwill Zwelithini, was not married or king yet. His mother, a teenage sweetheart of Zwelithini, died while giving birth. She was not of royal blood and, in fact, the family never revealed her identity. Not even Siboniso managed to find out. But the King would favour him above all of his kids and soon after Sib's birth, the King called his people together for a celebration. On that day, he held the baby high in his hands for all to see and said: "To you and the gods, I present my first son, your future king. I demand you to honour, protect, and obey him.

The Sangoma and I, your king, have bestowed the following names to him: Siboniso, Blekizizwe, and Londisizwe for protecting the nation."

They slaughtered a large bull for the occasion to share with all the people. The King's servants set up many tables loaded with food in the town's square for a feast celebrating Siboniso's birth.

Siboniso was a large baby, forecasting that he would grow to more than six feet or close to two meters tall. He had a handsome, open face with wide-set eyes. These eyes developed an exceptional quality when he got older. People would interpret them as commanding or even cruel. Some females found them alluring.

From an early age, he had a sort of aura that made people take notice. It was not that he pushed himself forward, but when he spoke, people took notice. By then, Sib had trained himself to think first before speaking by translating the question or the problem into two different languages in his head before he spoke.

After Siboniso's eighth birthday, his young life changed significantly. His father, the King, ordered his great-wife Mantfombi to bring Siboniso to an important meeting at his palace. As this was an unexpected request, Siboniso was rightfully nervous about it.

The King sat on his official throne and did not have his usual friendly smile for his oldest son. He looked Siboniso in the eye and said: "Boy, do you know my name?"

"Yes, *Ubaba* [Father], my king."

"Okay, tell me!"

"Goodwin Zwelithini kaBhekuzulu, son of King Cyprian Bhekuzulu Nyangayezizwe."

"And who was your great-great-grandfather?"

"The great king Shaka."

"Correct. He was the greatest Zulu king, King Shaka. Remember that. Do you know your names and their meaning? If you do, tell me!"

"Siboniso."

"Yes, and nothing more?"

"Bhekizizwe and Londisizwe. Siboniso means being a leader; Bhekizizwe and Londisizwe mean he protects the nation, in the generosity of spirit."

"Very good, my son; remember it and try to be true to your names."

Turning to Siboniso's stepmother, he said, "This boy is going to boarding school next week. Make sure that he knows that he is Zulu royalty and what we expect of him."

Chapter Three

So, after a hectic week of preparations for the departure to boarding school, the King's chauffeur picked up young Siboniso. Two of his older cousins were allowed to accompany him to the Stanger train station on the coast to catch the train to Durban.

At the station, they bought a train ticket for Siboniso. Both cousins had been to the same school and told him stories while they waited for the train to arrive. Listening to them would make you think the school would not want to enrol another royal family member. But, knowing them, Siboniso did not get scared but got even more excited to discover the new life that awaited him.

When the train arrived, they found him a place next to a window. They also asked the conductor to keep an eye on their relative and to ensure that he would disembark at the Durban Central Train Station. They assured him that somebody from the school would be waiting for him.

Sib waved goodbye for as long as he could see them, and then, for a bit, he felt very much alone and a bit scared. But soon, all kinds of people filled the cabin. There were whole families travelling together, and they had a merry time; they shared food and told stories. Siboniso started to enjoy himself and happily accepted some of the food that went around. He was hungrier than he thought.

The train whistled and puffed and sometimes went so fast that the scenery outside the window of mountains, forests and small villages passed by in a blur. Siboniso liked it best when the train slowed down for the next stop, giving him time to observe a South Africa he had never seen before.

The train halted at every station, but the time went quickly and, before he knew it, the conductor appeared, telling him to get off the train at the next stop.

Sib was one of many passengers who left the train. As instructed, he stayed put at the place where he disembarked. He had to tell himself not to get scared. *Be brave*, he told himself, *as a Zulu prince should be.*

To his relief, he did not have to 'be brave' for long as a man arrived carrying a cap on his curly black hair with the school's logo on it. He stopped in front of him and asked his name. His deep voice and friendly smile put Sib at ease.

When Siboniso said his name, he nodded happily. "That's it," he agreed. "That's the name of the new pupil I must pick up. Come with me, Siboniso. Do you want to sit in the front or the back?"

In the front, of course. Siboniso felt safe now and enjoyed the long drive to the school near Pietermaritzburg, about a ninety-minute drive inland from Durban.

Along the way, Sib asked the man, called Simon, many questions. Simon answered him as best as he could, but he looked aside and smiled when the questions stopped coming. Siboniso hadn't been able to keep himself awake. It had been a long day already.

The school consisted of many buildings and catered to primary and high school students from near and far. Nearly all pupils were boarders, sleeping in dormitories for the different age groups. Siboniso's father had six wives, resulting in a legion of half-brothers and -sisters for Siboniso. Additionally, all the cousins living in or around Nongoma meant that Sib was used to mixing with many children and had no trouble finding friends.

Boarding and school rules were firm but fair, with no special treatment for royal children. That suited Siboniso fine, and he soon fitted in.

Sib was a keen learner, and although he started in third grade, skipping a class took little time. He finished primary school after two more years.

———— ✦ ————

In the meantime, the royal family prepared for an exciting period. Close to his 10th birthday, the headmaster called him to his office. King Goodwill Zwelithini required Siboniso, his eldest son, to return home for the King's wedding to Princess Mantfombi of Swaziland. She would be Queen Mantfombi Dlamini, the Great Wife, as she was the only wife with royal blood.

This meant that Queen Mantfombi would be the most important of the royal wives and would have the final word in any disputes. Although she was not Sib's mother, he loved her like she was and called her *umama*. Of course, it was expected that Sib would attend the wedding, and he wanted to. The day arrived when Sib's favourite uncle, Prince Mangosuthu

Buthelezi (Sib called him Uncle Shenge) picked him up from school. He came in a sturdy 4×4 suited for the highway as well as the potholed roads of Zululand.

Siboniso was excited to see him and pelted him with questions about everything at home. During the long trip, they had time to talk. Queen Mantfombi had given birth to her first son shortly after Siboniso went to boarding school. He had been named Prince Misozulu, and now, as a two-year-old toddler, he would be the first in line to succeed the King.

"Do you realise that?" Uncle Shenge asked. "You will always be your father's favourite son, but this is our law."

"I know, Uncle, I know! I am glad the law says so. I never wanted to be king. I want to study and travel and choose the work I want to do."

It was an emotional reunion at the royal homestead. Everybody knew the King originally wanted Siboniso to be his successor. However, to marry Mantfombi, the daughter of the King of Swaziland, King Goodwin Zwelithini had to agree that their firstborn son would be the rightful heir to the crown.

The King explained the rules to Siboniso when he visited the King's quarters to pay his respects, and he was happy to hear that Siboniso felt a burden had lifted from his shoulders. The King then asked about school and Sib's dreams for the future.

Siboniso told him of his thirst for knowledge, especially about his nation's history and future. The King looked proudly at him and assured him the royal family would support him in all his endeavours.

It was still a week before the wedding and Sib had fun re-connecting with his friends, playing football and getting to know his little brother.

At the wedding, Siboniso had a prominent place among the royal family members but had no other role besides being there.

He was a keen observer. He was too young to be remembered by any of the leaders of the different African nations, tribes, and politicians, but he remembered names and appearances, including the white South African politicians who attended.

——— ✦ ———

After the wedding, Sib went back to school to continue his education. He was usually at the top of the class in all subjects and participated in sports, including rugby, but football remained his favourite. However, he did not strive to excel in any sport; he just saw it as a valuable tool for socialising and staying fit.

Sib was popular and well-respected by the other pupils at school, and this was not just because he was a prince. For instance, one day, close to finishing school, Siboniso saw a few boys bully a younger boy. This boy, thinly built and wearing glasses, was looking extremely uncomfortable. They pushed him around, and one of the bullies threw his schoolbag over the fence. Sib, already almost six feet tall and muscly from the regulated lifestyle and playing sports, assessed the situation and then called out, "Hey guys! I know who you are; you're in the year below my class. Do you want me to get you expelled?

Go and grab that bag and return it with apologies. Alternatively, you can take on me. I can easily flatten two cowards in one go."

The bullies took the wise option and sheepishly returned the bag. Before they disappeared, Siboniso warned them, "Attending this school means that you could become a leader of your people. Picking on a smaller person is not a good start!"

The boy called Mozes became Sib's friend for life.

Chapter Four

Siboniso was not just a goody-two-shoes. He liked to play practical jokes and was good at talking others into being allies. He often laughingly recalled a particular incident.

It had occurred during his junior years, when the boarding house master told them their dormitory needed renovation and directed them to relocate to the senior boys' sleeping quarters for two weeks. The older boys had more privacy. There were no dormitories, but a huge room divided by thin sheets of timber into several groups of four small spaces. Each boy had a bed, a tiny desk, a chest, and a curtain as a door. On top of each room's chest stood a metal pot with a lid. The sign stated: "Only to be used in emergencies."

About half of the spaces were unused, so the junior boys moved in. They loved their new privacy but were curious about the pot on the chest. They soon discovered it was not for cooking but for peeing if the bathroom was too far.

Well! After this revelation, the jokes kept coming … everyone seemed to have a pee joke to tell.

The pot was only to be used in emergencies, but they soon noticed that one of the senior boys was too lazy to walk to the bathroom and used it every night. Sib was a light sleeper and often woke up because of the clattering noise as the liquid fed into the metal pan.

So, Sib decided to play a practical joke. He got some mates together, and they concocted a plan. One of them had found a spool of fish line with which they secretly tied all the pots together. Sib was one of the main tie-ers.

That evening, they were all nervous, afraid that one of the seniors would notice the fish line, but nothing happened. Eventually, most of the boys fell asleep. Those who did not sleep heard the guy getting up and pulling his pot down. The resulting noise in the stillness of the night was deafening and awoke everybody, including their boarding house manager.

Sib owed up to being the instigator, but fortunately, management and most of the boys, including the senior boys, thought it was a great joke.

Still, Sib had to appear before the school director and explain what had happened. The director did not laugh and told him sternly never to repeat anything like that. He said that the catastrophic noise could have resulted in a panic attack in some boys or even a heart attack for the elderly manager.

The pots were a remnant of the dormitory's lack of a bathroom, and, after the incident, management removed them and confiscated the fishing line. Nevertheless, the story lived on in the school's annals.

— + —

The school years, where Sib felt protected and secure, were over too soon. Primary school and high school followed each other seamlessly. Sib's education had included two years at the mission school in Nongoma, with eight years at the boarding school. Sib finished his school years as one of the top students.

He returned home to his proud family for the summer holidays to celebrate his good results. He also wanted to discuss his plans for the future.

—— ✦ ——

Sib's plan to go to university in Johannesburg brought on a considerable dispute in the royal family. Some thought it would be fine if he could live with Mandela's family in Soweto. Although Nelson Mandela had been incarcerated on Robben Island since 1964, his family home was still in Soweto. Other family members argued that the long travel up and down to Wits, short for Witwatersrand University, would be too risky.

Soweto is a Johannesburg township, without much infrastructure or amenities. It was originally set aside by the government for residence by blacks, so they could work in Johannesburg while not being allowed to live there. Soweto grew into a sprawling township with many schools. In 1976, the then government made the Afrikaans language the mandatory language for teaching in schools, resulting in an uprising by the schoolkids. In a huge overreaction by the police, supported by the government, live ammunition was used and many kids were killed.

The Soweto uprising was fresh in the memory of Siboniso's family, and protests against the apartheid regime still regularly happened. The term 'apartheid' has been taken from the Afrikaans language and translates to 'separateness'. It came to mean a legal system of racial segregation.

It did not just mean that white men were the boss. Siboniso would have to get used to many rules, like not being allowed to travel in the same part of a bus or train and he would have to use a separate entrance to public buildings such as post offices.

Apartheid was enforced by the law throughout the country. And sometimes, outside of the law, by self-righteous Afrikaaners.

White people would be served in a shop before you, even if they entered it after you. There were other rules for people of mixed blood, which were less strict than for the Bantu. Asian people were called 'honorary whites' and awarded privileges, probably because they owned many of the small businesses essential to the country's economy. Interracial friendships were frowned upon, and such marriages were forbidden.

Siboniso was aware of this, but his life had been sheltered from the brutal effects of the regime. However, he was confident that going to university would give him tools to deal with apartheid and work for change.

———— ✦ ————

Several members of the royal family tried to get him interested in politics. It was during the time of the struggle for power between the Inkatha Freedom Party and the ANC, resulting in violent confrontations and killings in the KwaZulu territory. Even his father, the King, and Uncle Buthelezi, the founder of Inkatha, had heated discussions. It took a while for them to be convinced that Siboniso wanted nothing to do with politics. He wished to be a lawyer.

Even though Sib would never forget his blackness and hated apartheid, he would have to remain open to all views and stick to upholding the letter of the law. King Zwethelini reluctantly supported his son's choice.

Despite their political differences, King Zwethelini asked Uncle Buthelezi for help in finding accommodation for Siboniso, as he had many contacts in the big city.

Thanks to his high school results, Sib was accepted into Wits' prestigious law faculty. They only notified him one week before the course started, just when he had nearly given up hope.

Fortunately, Sib could move swiftly as only a few weeks before, the King had contacted Uncle Buthelezi, who invited Siboniso to his office in Johannesburg to sort out accommodation. Sib was keen to go.

Initially, the plan had been to visit Nelson Mandela's house in Soweto. By then, Aunt Winnie (Winnie Mandela—also a South African anti-apartheid activist and the second wife of Nelson Mandela) had been banished to the Orange Free State and would only return in 1985.

When Winnie heard that Siboniso was starting university (uni) at the same faculty in which her husband had studied, she offered Sib to stay in their house. By this time, Winnie and Nelson's two daughters had left home; one had completed a university course in the USA, and the other had married a Swazi prince.

It was a generous offer, and was considered by Siboniso, but he knew that travelling to uni would take time and effort.

Uncle Shenge had explained to Sib about the time Nelson Mandela had studied at Wits. He then had a family with young children, only making ends meet while juggling several jobs. The time wasted by travelling and the need for more quiet space had made studying hard for him. So, Sib was keen to find another place to stay.

Instead of going to Soweto, they had in mind another plan. They went to Nelson Mandela's office in Johannesburg; its location was not that far from Wits.

Even though Nelson was in jail, his office manager continued the law practice as best as possible. Buthelezi had never met him but knew his name was Manish Khan, of Indian heritage. Mr Khan was himself a lawyer and a study-mate of Mandela. His parents had been friends with Gandhi. When the security police arrested Mandela, his partner Thambo hid and fled the country soon after. Manish Khan, who was related to the owners of the building, went into hiding as well when they raided the office and confiscated or destroyed most of the contents.

Then, when Mandela was sentenced and disappeared into prison, Mr Khan returned to the office and tried to keep the practice going. His clients were Indians or blacks; nobody had much money, but he kept his head above water. However, the decade of the eighties was particularly brutal as clients were challenging to come by. Everybody was scared and tried to stay under the radar.

It was into this environment that Uncle Shenge and Sib arrived. They paused momentarily upon their arrival to admire the beautiful building containing the law office. Sadly, the inside could have been more attractive, as rooms and facilities had fallen into disrepair. Further, the paint had blistered, and doors were damaged or missing. But the two rooms Mr Khan occupied were clean and neat-looking, although scarcely furnished.

Mr Khan was friendly. He knew about Mr Buthelezi and was honoured to meet the founder of the Inkatha party. He also heard about Siboniso, son of the Zulu king, because he had regularly corresponded with Mr Nelson Mandela.

Sib told him that Aunt Winnie had invited him to stay in her house. He explained, however, that he had decided not to accept her offer, mainly because of the distance to the university campus and the chance of running into demonstrations and police brutality.

Sib looked at Mr Khan and said, "I was hoping that you might be able to suggest how to find a place to study in this city, preferably not too far from the Witwatersrand University."

Mr Khan understood the problem very well and, providing that Mandela agreed, he advised that he could offer one small office for Siboniso to study in, under the condition that he would fix up the room, repair what needed to be, and give it a new paint. He added that he would also have to pay a modest rent. Sib gladly accepted.

Satisfied that they had fixed Siboniso's problems, the two older men talked for a while about politics, the protests, and their fear of the brutal crackdowns by the police. However, they also spoke about their hope for the future, as the government had ordered Mandela's relocation to Cape Town. Sib listened to every word.

—— ✦ ——

At university, Sib had a pleasant encounter with Mozes, a friend from high school. In fact, he was the boy he had saved from the bullies.

"Sawubona! What are you doing here?" they both exclaimed.

"I study law, and you?"

"I am at the economic faculty," Mozes replied.

Sib clapped him on the shoulder: "Great to see you here! Let's have a drink and catch up."

Mozes had grown taller, though he was still more than a head shorter than Sib. The uni had a café for non-white people where they had a soft drink. Mozes explained why he had chosen to study economics.

"The whole world turns around money," he maintained. "I want to learn how to get rich! Not by studying law; too dry for me! Don't know how you do it."

"You are right," Sib laughed, "but when you guys run into trouble, you always come to the lawyers for help, right?"

"Yes, that is true, and then you ensure we never get rich."

Their talk flowed easily, and they shared many laughs. Mozes' thick glasses made him look like a dour bookkeeper, but his looks were deceiving; his sense of humour had Sib in stitches repeatedly. Their revived friendship would last throughout their lives.

Chapter Five

Sɪʙ ᴛᴏʟᴅ Mᴏᴢᴇs ᴀʙᴏᴜᴛ the building and the manager, Mr Khan, a lawyer friend of his uncle. He invited Mozes to go with him to check out the place where he had been secretly sleeping, as well.

"Wow, is that your uncle's name on the brass plate?" Mozes' mouth fell open when they arrived in the hall of the building. "Yes, that is my uncle, Nelson Mandela, my hero!"

"You never told me that your uncle was one of the ANC leaders and the biggest enemy of the government!"

"We can talk about that later. Let me introduce you to the man in charge here, Mr Khan."

Soon, the three of them were having coffee in the café next door that was run by an acquaintance of Mr Khan.

While sitting on the back terrace, Mr Khan said, "I have contacted your uncle Nelson. You can use the study room we agreed upon for a small rent and do errands for me when needed. He has also suggested using the small side room as a bedroom." He added with a wink, "I noticed that you have already started doing that."

Sib started to apologise, but Mr Khan waved him away. "Don't worry; it's okay."

After learning about Mozes' background and their friendship, Mr Khan said he thought there would be no problem if

Mozes wanted to join Sib. To their surprise, he added, "You can arrange to have some of your meals here, but you must discuss this with Mr Nick, the café owner. The back porch is for non-whites only, so I can't see any problem, or you can take meals to your room."

Mozes was keen to move in with Sib but still worried about their safety. He asked, "Sib, are you sure the police won't come raiding this building again? The government hates your uncle, even though he's in jail."

"Times are changing, Mozes," Sib reassured him. "Uncle Nelson is no longer on Robben Island; they moved him to a prison in Cape Town, last year. That must mean something. They sentenced him to life in prison. Not so much, I believe, because he was a leader in the ANC, but because he was a clever lawyer and worked against apartheid on many fronts. They called it 'sabotage'. His lot is one of the reasons that I try to keep out of politics."

———— ✦ ————

Sib and Mozes spent a few days cleaning and fixing up their rooms. In the other neglected rooms in the building, they each found an old desk and some chairs, which needed cleaning and minor repairs but were good enough to be used. Mattresses on the floor completed their new living arrangements.

Staying in an environment full of memories of lost and won human rights trials, combined with the buzz of present cases, taught Sib much about how a lawyer's world worked. He loved the atmosphere. When he had time, Mr Khan was always ready to talk shop. Sib usually spent most of his holidays in Johannesburg and worked for Mr Khan to gain as much experience as possible. He also regularly made the long trip home to report personally to his father, the King, and Queen Mantfombi. They wanted to stay informed about his progress and well-being.

As one of a few non-whites in a sea of white students, Sib found attending classes challenging. Apartheid was everywhere, even in the classroom. Siboniso tried to ignore it and concentrated on his studies.

As the years progressed, most students in his year came to respect and accept him as an equal because of his intellect, inborn tact, and good manners. He earned top marks in all subjects but never boasted about it.

As time went by, Sib's self-confidence increased. He flirted for a while with international law, but the extra burden would become too much. He decided to put this off until later.

He thought about the people that were important to him besides his parents. No one was more important than his uncles, Madiba and Shenge, and he aimed to make them all proud.

Chapter Six

IN THE FIRST YEAR OF HIS STUDY, Siboniso received a telegram from home that Chief Buthelezi's mother, Princess Magogo, was dying; he was required to join the family.

The Zulu people revered her; she was talented in the arts, a lover of music, and a composer of classical Zulu music. When Siboniso was growing up, he had spent time at her house during the school holidays to learn about the Zulu history in arts and music. She taught him the importance of culture and trained him to speak the African languages fluently. During that time, they had taken a shine to each other and her influence made him determined to promote and protect the Indigenous cultures throughout the African continent.

Sib had not lost a loved person before and her imminent passing deeply saddened him.

That night, he took the train, but he could not sleep a wink because the part of the train reserved for non-white people was very crowded. Whole families had already occupied the carriage with their kids, chickens, and even a goat. He spent most of the time standing in a corridor until, at the last stop before his, a family got out, and he quickly occupied one of their seats; but still, he gained no sleep.

One of his brothers was at the station yet, this time, there was no car but a horse. How long ago was it that Siboniso had been on a horse? Luckily, it was a docile animal. Sib wanted to go fast, but his brother reminded him that a horse could not urinate while walking. You had to give it a break now and then.

The long trip gave the brothers a chance to catch up. With an extended family like theirs, including their aunties, uncles and children, there was always gossip to share, which Sib had missed out on for a while. Most stories were good-natured and often funny, but this time, they mainly shared their memories of Aunt Magogo. His brother told him that most people were quiet and sad, as all deeply respected Aunt Magogo.

Upon their arrival, Sib was informed that King Zwelithini wanted to see him immediately, so Siboniso stopped at the palace first, even though he was so tired that he only wanted a bed.

His father embraced him and told him he had just learned that Princess Magogo had died in Durban. Her son, Uncle Shenge Buthelezi, would accompany her body to Nongoma for a traditional funeral, as she had requested. The burial would take place the day after tomorrow.

Father and son sat together without speaking, thinking of the woman that both of them called Aunt.

The King sighed and asked,

"Are you okay, my son? I know she had a special place in your heart."

Siboniso nodded, but his father noticed his slumped shoulders and the weary lines on his face. He immediately decided to send him to Queen Mantfombi's palace to rest.

"It's late, my son, and you have had a long day. Go to your mother, who eagerly awaits your arrival and will have your bed prepared. There is a lot of work tomorrow. I want you to offer Uncle Shenge any assistance he might need. We expect mourners to come from near and far; Aunt Magogo was loved by many."

Queen Mantfombi was happy the boy she cared for as a mother was home, even though the reason was sad.

She looked at him and said, "Every time I see you, you have grown a few centimetres more. My handsome son, have you fallen in love yet?"

Siboniso smiled shyly. With a shake of his head, he replied, "I have no time, my dear *umama*, but if I do, I'll bring her home to you to approve."

They talked a bit more about Aunt Magogo and Uncle Shenge, but Sib was very tired and his eyes wanted to keep closing. Soon, he retreated to his room, which was ready for him.

※

Over the next few exhausting days, thousands of mourners visited the town of Nongoma. They occupied every available accommodation and even camped in the open. Friends and family filled the palaces of the King's six wives and the Buthelezi residences.

During this time, Sib was surprised to meet a fellow student from Wits who studied literature. They once had had a casual conversation at the non-white cafe, where they found a common interest in the future of art by black artists.

His name was Bhekizizwe Peterson, and he revealed that he was a big fan of Princess Magogo's work. He was attending the funeral to pay his respects. Even though Bhekizizwe was a mature-age student, they both remembered their conversation. For Siboniso, Bhekizizwe would become a role model in the way Aunty Magogo had been.

After assisting and attending several ceremonies, including the burial of his beloved aunt, Sib was relieved to be able to return to his life in Johannesburg.

— ✦ —

Then, in 1985, Aunt Winnie Mandela's banishment was lifted, and she was allowed to return home. Siboniso visited her once, but he did not like her advocating an armed struggle. It seemed contrary to the teachings of his uncle.

Winnie continuously tried to recruit him, which was enough for Sib to begin avoiding her. He was trying to complete his lawyer's degree that year, so he had a good excuse.

— ✦ —

Siboniso graduated as a trainee lawyer with honours. Mr Khan told Sib that he had consulted Mr Mandela, and they had agreed to offer Siboniso a junior position in the lawyer's firm for a basic salary.

Enthusiastically, Sib accepted and started three years of practice under the supervision of Mr Khan. He was lucky to have a good relationship with his employer and received good guidance. The job was not overly exciting, as Sib had to do a lot of reading and research concerning Mr Khan's cases. Still, he realised that he was lucky. From his peers, he learned that established lawyers used their junior ones as cheap labour, keeping them working for long hours with little pay.

— ✦ —

Often, when Sib delivered a research report to his boss, Mr Khan asked him for his thoughts. Both enjoyed the discussions that followed. It was good practice. He also learned a lot when he accompanied Mr Khan to court. Sometimes, Sib commented that the prosecutor did not speak the truth or that the judge had made a mistake. Mr Khan usually replied, "Even if you are right, you don't argue with a judge."

If Sib protested, he would say, "You must remember that, when in court, the judge is always right. Is that clear? Always! You might be sure he is not, my young friend, but take it from me, would a judge admit to being wrong?

He will never admit that to a young lawyer."

"You mean to a black lawyer?"

"No, Sib, not to any young inexperienced lawyer. When you are an established lawyer and know the judge, you could try diplomatically, but certainly not during a court session. If you would try it as an apprentice lawyer, he will make mincemeat of you and your reputation."

Chapter Seven

Siboniso's first case came when he was still an apprentice. It occurred when Mr Khan phoned in early to tell Sib there was a green file on his desk. He said, "Study it. You know the case. Make sure you will be on time in court and tell the judge that I am not well today and have appointed you to defend Mr Mosi Keita."

"Who is the judge? Do you know?"

"Yes, I know, it is Judge Van der Merwe. He can be difficult occasionally, but he is fair. I know you can do it. Good luck."

Sib remembered the distraught man standing in the hall of the building the day before, pleading to talk to a lawyer. Mr Khan had spent a long time with him in his office and had managed to calm him down. He told Sib that Mosi Keita's 16-year-old son, Simba, had been arrested and detained in Security Headquarters at John Vorster Square. Simba had participated in the student protests against apartheid. His father had been so upset that he had not known where he was going. Unwittingly, he had wandered into a whites-only area, where he was soon arrested and charged with infiltrating a white area without a permit. Sib ensured he arrived at the court early enough to present his credentials and inform the judge that Mr Khan was ill. He had stayed up until midnight studying the judgements of similar cases in the past, preparing his defence. It was his first case. He wanted it to be a success, for himself and for Mosi.

Walking into the courtroom and feeling a bit self-conscious, Sib greeted his client courteously and settled his tall frame into the next chair, telling him not to worry. The court clerk read the charge of trying to infiltrate a white-only area for unknown purposes.

The police officer who arrested Mosi told the judge that he had walked past Mosi sitting on a bench and crying. He had no license to be there and refused to answer questions, so he had taken him to the station and charged him.

Sib stood up, asking permission to speak.

"Permission granted," the judge intoned.

Siboniso, looking impressive in his long black gown and white collar, nodded and, turning around, told the accused to stand up and answer all his questions honestly.

Through his gentle questioning, Siboniso managed to get the frightened man to open up. Mosi Keita told the court that he had gone to town to persuade his son Simba to return home with him. Unfortunately, he had arrived at the protest at the same time as the police charged on the students, using teargas and sticks.

"They rounded up several students, including Simba," Mosi explained, "and took them to John Vorster Square. Ambulances picked up the ones that didn't get up, whether they were wounded or dead. I didn't know." Mosi Keita's voice broke at this point as he revealed how he had then gone to the prison requesting access to his son. They chased him away, threatening to arrest him too.

After telling Mosi Keita to sit down, Siboniso turned to address the judge. "Your Honour, the accused, Mosi Keita, has been charged with infiltrating a white-only area for an unknown purpose. As you just heard, he wasn't aware of his surroundings. The worry about his son prevented him from thinking straight. He looked for a place to sit and recover enough to undertake the journey home to Soweto, where he would have to tell his family what happened. Mr Keita has two more kids and needs to provide for his family; he has already lost two days' pay. As he has never been charged or convicted of any crime, I plead in his name for mercy."

To Siboniso's relief, Judge Van der Merwe agreed with him and dismissed the charges without further ado.

In the corridors of the Court House, the judge stopped Sib on the way out. "I noticed you are a junior lawyer. You did well!"

The compliment brought a smile to Siboniso's lips. It still showed when he stepped into the office. Mr Khan, who had arrived in the meantime, noticed.

"Tell me," he said, "it went well, didn't it?"

"Case dismissed, of course," Sib announced, explaining how the court case had gone.

But his smile had disappeared, as he was thinking about Simba, Mosi Keito's son and the other school kids. It was Sib's first confrontation with the frightening crackdown on dissent in South Africa. John Vorster Square's Security Office had a reputation for torture and suspicious deaths of prisoners.

These thoughts prompted Mr Khan and Sib, joined by

Mozes, to have intense discussions, not just on that day but going forward. This began to make Siboniso rethink his wish to stay out of politics.

A few days later, Mr Khan relayed a message from Nelson Mandela congratulating Siboniso on completing his studies and wishing him well. Mr Mandela also wrote that he was happy with Sib and Mozes' living arrangements for the time being.

"Thank you, Mr Khan," stated Siboniso. "It is great to hear from him, but why does he say, 'for the time being'?"

"Well," Mr Khan replied with a big smile, his glasses misting up from emotion, which was very unusual for the stoic lawyer, "We are slightly convinced that the government might release our leader soon. International pressure is mounting, and the economy suffers badly because of all the embargoes and sanctions. Views and politics are changing in SA. Imagine my friends, we might see the end of apartheid!"

— ✦ —

This optimism invaded their attitude toward life and the discussions of their future plans. One evening, Mozes, who had recently started his practice year at one of the big banks, asked Sib, "What is your real goal in life? Is it to become a prominent lawyer like your uncle? You know my goal; I would like to get rich by playing the markets, but what about you?"

"Well, my friend, I am going to tell you, but you must promise that, for the time being, this stays between us."

"Promise."

"Firstly," Sib said with a wink, "I want to test your general knowledge about the world, apart from the economics."

"Okay, go ahead."

"How many states are there in the US?"

"About forty, I think."

"Fifty, plus some islands. How many countries are on our continent—Africa?"

"About fifty? Not 100% sure."

"Fifty-four, you are close. In your opinion, what is a significant difference between the USA and Africa?"

"Africa is larger, but the USA is rich and strong, and Africa is poor."

"Larger, yes, about four times, but what does the USA have that Africa has not?"

"What do you mean?"

"Well, the US doesn't have more workers. We have about a billion more people. It doesn't have more minerals. We have gold, diamonds, oil, and other resources!"

"What the heck are you on about, Mr Siboniso?"

Mozes queried watching his friend intently.

"I want to prove to you that the USA is rich and robust, as you said, because they have one government, and we are all divided. Not only are we divided because of the legacy of colonialism but also because of different religions and tribes and a deep mistrust of each other. Apartheid is regulated by law in South Africa but practised by many people worldwide, also in Africa. The lighter your skin, the better your chances to succeed in life.

"My goal is to make us one, independent of colour or religion. We could be one of the best, richest and most potent continents in this world, and if we do it right, everybody could have a decent life. We need a united nations of Africa!"

"Wow!" Mozes exclaimed. "You are aiming high!"

"Yes, and you must help me because this will cost much money, time, and dedication. You and I must start by keeping our ears and eyes open for people with similar ideas. There are students from other African countries at uni. Admittedly," Siboniso said with a shrug, "many are white or part white, but there is a good chance that they will be part of the future leadership of their countries.

"We both still need to attend uni to see our supervisors during the practice years. Let's talk to these students and gather as much information about every African country as possible. We need to know what makes them tick, their direction of politics, religion, and where the money comes from."

"Do you think rulers of African countries will give up their power and independence for your new plan?"

"Good question. No, they don't have to. The different US states keep much of their liberty, but you're right; one of the biggest challenges will be to convince them they won't lose their independence. We need to know their leaders' strong and weak points and what keeps them in power."

Chapter Eight

With all these ideas swirling through his mind, Siboniso did not concentrate sufficiently on his work; even Mr Khan noticed it. So, he came up with a new concept. The building behind theirs—a hotel for non-whites—had a swimming pool, and he organised with the owner that Sib and Mozes could swim there in the early mornings.

"Listen," he said, "young men should not be holed up all day. Exercise to clear your mind; that's what you need!"

The young professionals appreciated Mr Khan's initiative and thoroughly used the opportunity. They now had the best environment for work and study; Siboniso even started a course in international law.

During a long weekend, Sib visited Aunt Winnie in Soweto. Mrs Mandela said she had had another visit from the police.

"They made a mess of the house but found nothing incriminating." She smiled triumphantly as she stated this.

Aunt Winnie talked about her hopes for Uncle Nelson's freedom and tried again to recruit Sib for her cause, to no avail. After the visit, Sib boarded a bus back to Johannesburg at the same time as a white lady. He stepped back and let her go first but thought it strange that she would travel on a bus for non-whites.

At his stop, Sib got off the bus, and so did the lady. Siboniso went on his way even though she called after him in the
Afrikaans language to stop.

Sib just continued, but she caught up with him and said,
"*He swart ou, kan jy nie hoor nie?*" [Hé! Black guy, can't you
hear?] "I could not imagine a nice lady like you would shout
like that." Taken aback by that unexpected answer, she said,
"*Ek het gesê om te stop en vir my te wag*!" [I said to stop and
wait for me.]

Lady! I study here at the Witwatersrand University, *en
ek kan jou taal praat* [and I can speak your language], but I
prefer English if you don't mind. And, if I am right, this is a
two-language country."

"*Jou slimkop*! [You smartass!] Show me your papers!"

Siboniso was getting annoyed, but told himself to stay calm
and comply. He extracted his identity pass from his wallet, well
aware that it identified him as the son of the present Zulu king.

The policewoman—that was what Sib discovered she was
when he spotted her identity tag on her collar—studied the pass.
With raised eyebrows, she appeared to be slightly impressed.

"And you have no further papers on you? You know I can
strip search you here and now."

"I know you can and might like it, but not here. At your
office, a male officer would have to do it; it would be no fun
for either of us."

"You … smart-ass!" she gasped. "You better watch your
words! What are you studying at uni?"

"Law, and I aim to become a good lawyer like my uncle,

Nelson Mandela."

"In your pass, it said you are a Zulu. Mandela is no Zulu. How can he be your uncle?"

"Madam, in our community, if you know and deeply respect someone, he becomes your family, but I suppose you cannot understand that."

"You need to become a brilliant lawyer because if you keep visiting that woman in Soweto, you might end up at Robben Island, like her husband," she growled. "*Daar is nog baie plek*!" [There is still a lot of room]. With that warning, she gave the pass back and walked away.

When Sib told him about the encounter, Mozes said: "She obviously kept Winnie's house under surveyance. Glad you kept your calm but you should train harder with swimming," he teased. "Robben Island is a fair distance from the mainland, and the water is cold, too." They both had a good laugh.

—— ✦ ——

As time went on, Siboniso succeeded in roping Mozes in as a partner in his ambitious plan of uniting Africa. However, Mozes became disheartened when he discovered they were not the first.

"Sib, did you know that an 'Organisation of African Unity' exists? They are more or less doing what we want to do."

"I know," Sib nodded, "and that will be an enormous help to us, as their ground rules are there, and their offices established. However, they mainly work on cooperation and mediation concerning war or disputes between members or dealing with the consequences of colonialism.

"Our plans go further than that; we want to make Africa one. Did you know some countries started this organisation with the same idea as ours in 1963? It never rose adequately from the ground. Let's work with them once we decide on the path to follow.

"Something else; I am going to introduce you to a new friend."

"And who may that be, and from what African country is he?"

"The only thing you have right is that it is a male. Let me explain. A couple of weeks ago, when I was in the supermarket, a black man with an American accent had a problem, and I assisted him. We started to talk and had a coffee; he is a computer programmer at the American Consulate here and a sympathetic person. He told me that when the US government offered him the job, he accepted it because he was interested in how apartheid worked here in South Africa, compared to race relations in his own country."

"And does he like it here?" asked Mozes.

"You can ask him that yourself, as he will be here Wednesday afternoon. His name is Frank."

That Wednesday, the threesome met at the back terrace of the restaurant next door. After introductions, they shared a drink, and after Mozes' question, Frank explained that it was not only the system of apartheid that interested him but also his heritage that motivated him.

Frank went on to reveal that his mother had dual nationality, just like him, as he was born in Nigeria. However, he had only spent his first year there when his American father worked at the Consulate in Lagos. He was eager to learn more about Africa.

"Is there sufficient work for you here?"

"Oh yes, the computer technology in the States is top of the world and all friendly embassies and consulates can call upon me. Computer knowledge in South Africa is still so new that I get inundated with requests for advice."

Frank told them that the US had recently changed its political position towards South Africa because before, the ANC had been leaning towards communism, but that had changed.

"That is because Sib's uncle is one of the top men in the ANC," Mozes contributed.

"Is that so, Sib? Tell me more."

"Yes, Mozes is right. He is not directly family but he is a revered family friend I call uncle. Nelson Mandela's office is right next door. Haven't you heard of him? They arrested and jailed him more than twenty years ago."

"Yes, of course, I have heard of him," Frank nodded. "But remind me why they arrested him."

"My uncle is a lawyer and an activist. He was campaigning against the apartheid regime. His growing support was threatening to the government, so they called his peaceful activism 'sabotage' and jailed him for life. But his support keeps escalating globally, and the pressure on the government is growing to release him. Fingers crossed!"

"Is there no apartheid in America?" asked Mozes.

"Oh yes, there is, even if not by law." Frank answered, adding, "There is more of this racist behaviour in the south than in the north of the country, but it is everywhere, and as a black person, you never know what to expect. At least here in your country, you know where you stand, although I would hate to be subjected to it constantly."

Chapter Nine

A COUPLE OF WEEKS LATER, Frank called Sib. "We are having a party tomorrow night. Do you guys want to join us?"

"What is the occasion? Do we have to dress up for it?"

"No, man, just casually. The occasion is the birthday of the first American president, George Washington, and it is supposed to be a great party with a jazz band from the States."

"Well, count me in, but Mozes, who is here with me, says he has to decline. Regrettably, he has another engagement planned."

It was an animated party, and the friends had a lot to discuss. Frank introduced Sib to people who he knew would be good to know if he wanted to progress his 'unity' plans.

The band was not only fantastic, but they also had an outstanding and attractive female singer called Jessie. Jessie moved sensually on the rhythm of the music, dancing through the room, stopping at a table occasionally, making eye contact with people in the audience, including Frank and Siboniso. Sib felt melancholic, as he sang along with the old Negro spirituals, and as each song concluded, he applauded enthusiastically.

After the band had finished, Frank invited the singer to have a drink at their table. They had a fun time talking about their home country, be it that Jessie's eyes often met with Sib's.

Jessie asked Sib if he had enjoyed the music. He responded that her singing touched him deeply, especially the spirituals about the Negroes' pain and suffering. He complimented her on her beautiful voice and wondered if there would be a recording he could buy.

As the evening went on, Jessie appeared genuinely interested in Siboniso and asked what he was doing. She smiled when he replied, "I'm just a junior lawyer."

Frank immediately interrupted. "He is not just a junior lawyer; he is also of royal blood, and his uncle is Nelson Mandela."

Sib felt uncomfortable with the attention he suddenly received and soon found excuses to leave the party.

During a long weekend, Sib decided to visit friends in Soweto, including Aunt Winnie. However, there was a problem with the buses, as they had recently stopped being available for black people. Therefore, Siboniso signalled to a taxi. The taxi driver—one of the so-called 'honorary' whites—did not like to take a black person and revealed that he did not feel like driving to an address in Soweto.

"I'll have to charge you extra," he announced.

"Is that because you feel unsafe there?"

"No. It's because of the bad state of the roads. I have to look after my beautiful car."

Sib thought the car was at least fifteen years old and commented, "Most workers here at the Rand come from Soweto, and they pay taxes. Fancy that, there is no money for the roads where they live."

The driver was quick to respond. "10% tax from the lowest wages is not much."

"That's right," Sib agreed. "They need a pay rise! But it is no reason to neglect their roads."

He did not want the driver to know where he was going, so he intended to get off well before Winnie's house. However, they never got there anyway, as they had to stop for an accident outside Soweto.

Sib knew that it could take some time to clear, so he stepped out of the car and went to have a look. The ambulance with two paramedics had just arrived. One black person was on the ground, bleeding from his head, but the paramedics had ignored him and instead, went to the two white people in the car. It looked like one person's leg was broken and one possible whiplash.

Sib could not believe his eyes when the white people were helped into the ambulance while the bleeding man was just left lying on the ground.

Before they could drive away, Siboniso stepped in and, pointing to the injured black man, asked, "What about that patient?" "You have to call the non-white hospital. Not our job!"

Trying to control his rising anger, Sib demanded, "Give me at least a bandage to stop the bleeding and some antiseptic."

They did as he asked, and Sib disinfected the wound and put the first-aid bandage on the man's head wound. Then he called over to the taxi driver,

"Help me get this poor man into your taxi so we can take him to Baragwanath Hospital."

"No way!" exclaimed the driver. "I am not an ambulance. I can't take him in my car. I will never get the bloodstains out."

By now, Siboniso was truly angry. He grabbed the driver's neck with his right hand and snatched the key out of the ignition with his left.

"I'll be back," he growled at the driver. "If you have a blanket or something else, spread it on the back seat."

Sib gestured to the audience that had assembled on the sidewalk, asking them for assistance. Immediately, three of them stepped out to help. Their response restored Sib's faith in humanity, calming him down.

Between the four of them, they efficiently carried the wounded man to the car and carefully placed him on the back seat that was now covered in a sheet.

After thanking his helpers, Sib took down the contact details of a witness. He also wrote down the number plate of the damaged car, before instructing the driver to take them to the hospital.

During the trip, Siboniso talked soothingly to the frightened man, assuring him they would look after him at the hospital and let his family know.

Sib had already taken down the injured man's name and address as he had a thought about initiating a court case. The head wound didn't look too serious, but it needed stitches.

The driver kept complaining, but he delivered them to the hospital. Upon their arrival, some first-aiders immediately cared for the patient at the hospital's emergency entrance.

"Would you please fill in some paperwork?" they requested.

"I don't know the man," Sib advised. "We picked him up at an accident. But okay, I'll just be a moment. I need to pay for the taxi."

He had realised that he would not be able to go to any of his proposed visits. He certainly did not want to show up in his bloodstained clothes!

When Sib returned to the man on the stretcher, one of the nurses directed him to the administration office. Once there, he reported how he had been in a taxi, and they had to stop for the accident. He went on to explain what had happened and provided the car's registration number. After more wasted time waiting around, they let him go. He left his contact details behind before taking a taxi back home.

This time, the taxi driver was friendly. He noticed the bloodstains on Sib's jacket and shirt, and he was concerned. Sib told him what had happened, and during the ride home, they talked about the lack of services for non-whites and their hopes for a change in government.

As the taxi driver happened to live near Winnie Mandela, he commented that she had returned home. He also wondered if her husband was about to be set free, as it was now common knowledge that the government had moved Nelson Mandela from Robben Island to a Cape Town prison.

"That has to mean something," he mused. "What do you think?"

Siboniso confirmed that he had had the same thoughts and hopes, but he did not reveal his connection to the Mandela family. However, he gave the driver extra money and the address of the patient with the request to tell his family that he had been admitted to hospital but was not seriously wounded.

When he arrived home, he told Mozes about the accident,

and the recounting made him angry, once again.

"I intend to write about it to the newspapers. Apartheid is one thing, but this disrespect for a human life is disgusting."

Mozes managed to talk him out of it by arguing that attracting attention to himself would not be very smart. "Anyway," he added, "most of the South African newspapers would not even consider printing it."

Chapter Ten

ONE FRIDAY MORNING IN 1990, Mr Khan had news for them, confirming the rumours.

President de Klerk had announced that Nelson Mandela would be set free on the eleventh of February. It was eight years after he had been moved from Robben Island to a Cape Town prison.

Shortly after, they received a letter with an invitation to attend his first freedom speech. On the invitation, Mandela had written: "See you soon!"

Winnie Mandela had travelled to Cape Town and accompanied her husband when he left prison. Security guards drove them to Cape Town City Hall, where thousands of supporters had assembled, waiting for Nelson Mandela's first speech as a free man.

Mr Khan, Siboniso, and Mozes, who had travelled down south to the beautiful coastal city of Cape Town, found an excellent place to listen but kept away from the forefront that was reserved for active ANC members.

Nevertheless, Aunt Winnie spotted Sib because of his height and pointed him out to her husband. Nelson Mandela waved at him, and also noticed his old friend, Manish Khan.

The audience listened spellbound to Mandela's speech, which was shared worldwide. He did not talk about his suffering but acknowledged the suffering of many under the apartheid regime. He assured them that he had not done any deals with the government. However, he revealed that he had demanded that negotiations between the government and the ANC leadership would take place to end apartheid and achieve peace for all races.

Nelson Mandela used his speech to thank everyone, including student groups of all ages, workers, mothers and fathers, political groups and others, for their continued struggle against injustice. Mandela's impassioned plea encouraged everyone to continue their activism until negotiations were complete and elections called. Mandela added that they must be optimistic about the future and how they would make this a fair nation for everyone.

— ✦ —

After the speech, Sib, Mozes and Mr Khan managed to get through the crowd to shake Mandela's hand. All three pledged their full support to their leader. There was no time for more, as many people sought Mandela's attention. They had business and work to attend to anyhow, and it called them back to Johannesburg.

— ✦ —

Not long after this significant occasion, Siboniso was delighted to see Mr Mandela stepping into his office. With a big hug, Sib asked, "What are you doing here, Madiba?" Madiba is the name of the Thembu clan to which Mandela belonged. When Mandela is called Madiba, it is meant to show respect and affection.

"Can't I visit my own office, please?" Mandela asked.

"Oh! I am so sorry. What am I saying? I will vacate your office straight away, Uncle."

"That won't be necessary," Mandela laughed. "I will not be back here to work. It was great to see you in Cape Town and to meet your friend Mozes."

He gave a friendly nod to Mozes, who jumped up to shake his hand and said how honoured he was to meet Mr Mandela.

"I take it you two made this your office and living quarters? You have fixed it up nicely! Let's go to Mr Khan's office, and then we can talk."

It was an emotional reunion between the two friends who had not seen each other for twenty-seven years, apart from the brief encounter in Cape Town. They shared dinner on the back porch of the café next door.

They all had so many questions that Mandela raised his hands. "Hé! Man! I am not in court, you know, one at a time, please." After he had answered a few of Mr Khan's questions, it was Sib's turn.

"After so many years in prison, Madiba, please tell me how you managed to deliver such a beautiful speech without a word of blame, hate, or aggression. Are you a saint?"

"No, my boy," Mandela smiled. "I am not a saint; I had twenty-seven years to think about a strategy to achieve healing and peace. I concluded that blame, condemnation, and revenge would lead us nowhere. You must realise that most white South African people under forty-five are born under the apartheid regime and don't know better. They feel safe and comfortable; servants and workers are cheap. Except for a progressive minority, they do not want to change. They have the power, the law, and the guns. Black power scares them, so a positive stand without blame makes progress possible.

"Now, after answering your questions, I have some of myself. Sib and Mozes, what are your plans for the future?"

Sib went first. "Madiba, as you know, my father, the King, is often short of money. He has six wives and palaces, the education of twenty-eight children, and expensive hobbies. Being king brings in large funds, but maintaining his status is also costly. Therefore, I provide for myself as much as possible. Thank you for allowing Mr Khan to offer us a place to live and study here for a low rent. That was and is an immense help.

"After finishing my studies and now in my practice years, I also started on a master's degree in international law. However, studying is taking up much of my time, while Mr Khan is getting busier. I can give up the study, and if Mr Khan agrees, I can stay and work for him full time after completing my practice years."

"No way, Siboniso!" exclaimed Mandela. "I don't think your heart is in that plan. It did not come over as very enthusiastic. Please continue to study; I will need your expertise in international law.

"If my information is right, the ANC will own the Shell Building here in Johannesburg shortly and make it their headquarters. And once I have an office, I want you to be close. You should know that I already received many invitations to speak about my experience and views, and I would like you to assist me, whenever Mr Khan can spare you. What do you think?"

"Wow, thank you, Uncle," Sib blurted out with shining eyes. "There is nothing that I would rather do."

"And what about you, young Mozes?"

"Madiba, if I may call you that, my degree in economics got me a position at a bank, but my heart isn't in it. I intended to get rich, but with a friend like Siboniso, that is very unlikely."

"Well, get as much experience as you can, then we might call on your knowledge to assist us in managing our finances. But be aware that associating with the ANC will not bring riches either!"

———— + ————

Two months later, Mandela travelled to London to give a speech at the Wembley Charity Concert. Millions of people watched the sold-out music show at Wembley Stadium and listened to Mandela's gripping speech in which he announced that the abolishment of the apartheid regime was close. The speech was globally broadcast via television and radio programs.

It was the first time Siboniso had travelled with his idol, and it made an indelible impression on him.

[Unfortunately, at the end of 1993, Sib could not accompany Mandela to Oslo for the Nobel Peace Prize he shared with Prime Minister De Klerk. Winnie Mandela was also absent as Nelson and Winnie disagreed strongly on the way forward to dismantling apartheid. Their 38-year marriage ended first in separation in 1992 and in divorce in 1996. In 1998 Mandela married his third wife, Graça Machel, the widow of the former president of Mozambique and enjoyed happy and peaceful years with her until his death in 2013.]

Then, at a national ANC meeting, the ANC officially took possession of the Shell Building, where its offices were until the 1994 general elections. Overwhelmingly, the people of South Africa chose the ANC party to lead the government and Nelson Mandela as their president. He was to be the first black ruler of South Africa, and his appointment made headlines the world over. South Africa was celebrating, especially the long oppressed black people. But also, most other South Africans, as they believed in Nelson Mandela's message of reconciliation.

There was tremendous goodwill among all races, but the baggage was huge, and the hurt inflicted not easy to heal.

———— + ————

During the election year, Siboniso completed his master's degree in international law. He made himself available to assist Mandela in any way required while continuing to stay with Mozes at Mr Khan's offices and occasionally doing work for him.

Even before he was elected as leader of the ANC, Mandela hit the ground running. He initiated the Truth and Reconciliation Process and travelled near and far to speak about peace and cooperation between nations. He travelled to many African and several overseas countries. The people flocked to hear him everywhere and were inspired by his message of peace, justice, and forgiveness.

Siboniso accompanied him on some of these trips and met people whose cooperation he would later seek to promote his vision for Africa. He worked as an advisor for Mandela on his visits to Rhodesia, Zambia, Libya, and Algeria.

Chapter Eleven

MANDELA ATTENDED A FEW more functions in the UK before flying to Ethiopia, the last stop of his trip. Siboniso flew back to Johannesburg, but only for a short time. One of Mandela's aides contacted him, saying, "Please, get on a plane to Addis Ababa because our leader has left his speech at home."

Sib managed to book the last seat in business class with a copy of the talk to which he had contributed. He greeted the person sitting next to him and started re-reading the draft. Sib could see that the man beside him was studying papers from an international mining company. Siboniso showed his interest, and after introducing themselves, they started a conversation about mining and the change of government in South Africa.

His neighbour's name was Imari. He told Sib he had been born in Cape Town to an Indian father and a mother of mixed race. He had enjoyed a privileged upbringing, studied in the UK, and had not suffered under apartheid like his family.

"Did you study mining at uni?" Siboniso asked.

"Yes, I did. A double degree in mining engineering and business administration. Four years ago, a multinational mining company based in the United Kingdom employed me as a consultant to improve safety regulations and cooperation in mining."

"Are there mines in Ethiopia, or is that an in-between stop?"

"There are mines in Ethiopia, as in many African countries. They are not on the scale of the South African ones in size and safety management. Nevertheless, I am particularly focused on the safety management of our mines and am due to report back to the UK." He looked keenly at Siboniso before asking, "And what are you planning to do in Addis Ababa, if I may ask?"

Sib told Imari that he was an aide to ANC leader Nelson Mandela, who would be addressing the government of Ethiopia but that he had left his speech behind. They both had a bit of a laugh and shook their heads.

Siboniso opened up about his youth as a Zulu prince and rude awakening to the apartheid regime when he had moved to Johannesburg to study law.

Comparing experiences in student life and their work provided so much stuff to discuss that the flight seemed too short. However, as the plane landed, they exchanged contact details and promised to catch up when possible.

At the last moment, Imari said, "Sib, if you can break away after Mandela's speech, there is a social function at the Chamber of Commerce. It will be a good opportunity to meet influential people." And he handed him an invitation card. "Use this card, and you will get in."

After another well-received speech from Mandela, Siboniso slipped away and attended the function without any problems. Imari introduced him to several dignitaries, including a young lady named Makeda and her brother, Aman.

It was a classic case of 'love at first sight' between Makeda and Sib. They kept eye contact whenever they could and, later that night, Imari, who was amused to be a witness to the sparks flying between the star-struck couple, managed to find them a quiet place to sit and talk, even though the girl's older brother was her chaperone. Imari was a family friend and managed to distract Aman while the two of them walked away, giving the couple some privacy.

They held hands and didn't stop talking, confessing their strong feelings for each other. Both commented that even though it must seem ridiculous to outsiders, they were sure they had met the love of their lives.

Sib wanted to know everything about her life, and she told him that she came from a royal family, prominent in the largest tribe of Ethiopia. Her name, Makeda, translated as 'the beautiful', after the Queen of Sheba.

She explained that Ethiopians believe that their first king was the son of King Solomon and the Queen of Sheba, who ruled over Egypt and Ethiopia. While she was talking, Sib was drawn to her beauty. Her pitch-black hair was braided into a complicated hairdo that gracefully framed her heart-shaped face. The wide-set dark eyes and a generous mouth completed the picture.

Siboniso told her that he too came from a royal family.

Now and then, Makeda broke out in laughter, listening to his stories about growing up in Nangoma. Siboniso was mesmerised by her sparkling eyes and fully agreed with the meaning of her name. He knew that this was the girl he wanted to share his life with.

Comparing their experiences growing up as royalty, Sib learnt that Makeda had gone to an international boarding school in Europe and spoke four European languages fluently, on top of a few Ethiopian ones. Sib was very impressed, but she said it was not much, as Ethiopia has more than eighty tribes, each with its own language. She had a diplomat uncle who spoke at least twelve on top of English, German, and French.

Just before her brother returned with Imari, they exchanged contact details and promised to wait for each other and write as often as possible. Siboniso assured her he would save as much as he could and visit her family within a year, maybe two, to ask her father for her hand.

Shortly after, Aman and Imari joined them. After a bit of polite chitchat, Makeda had to leave with her escort.

Sib felt relieved that Imari had plenty of people to talk to because his heart wasn't in it anymore. He left soon after.

———— + ————

On their flight back to Johannesburg, Nelson Mandela told Siboniso that he liked Ethiopia more than any other country they had visited.

When Sib enthusiastically agreed, he asked,

"Tell me your reasons, Sib, as I didn't see much of you after my speech. You told me you were going to the Chamber of Commerce function with somebody you met on the plane. How was that?"

"Yes, Madiba, I will tell you about Imari later, but first of all, I met Makeda, the most beautiful and exceptional young lady I have ever known. I am head over heels in love with her. She feels the same about me; is that not crazy? She belongs to one of the royal families, but it wouldn't make any difference where she came from. I cannot stop thinking about her!”

Mandela smiled. “That’s not so crazy; it happens to many young and not-so-young people. Congratulations, what are the plans?”

“We have no concrete plans yet, but we have promised to wait for each other till I have the funds to front up to Makeda’s father and ask his permission to marry her. Oh, Madiba, I am so happy.”

Mandela was delighted for him and offered to help if needed to make this happen.

He then asked him about his future work plans.

“Uncle, I have wanted to tell you my ambitions for a long time. We have so little time for a private conversation, but this is as good a time as ever. I want to stay as your advisor on international trips and work for Mr Khan when needed.

“Apart from that, I dream of making the whole of Africa one, like the United States of America. Did you know that Africa is about four times bigger than the US, that we have about a billion more people, and that we produce half of all the gold in the world? Also, Africa produces most diamonds and nearly all the minerals we need!”

“I am not often speechless, boy, but that is a big dream. However, if anybody can achieve it, I know it is you.”

“I am only extending your dream, Uncle.”

“Only, you say! How do you think you’ll realise this dream, my friend? Is this why you pursued your master’s degree in international law? I must say, I did notice you reminding me to mention international cooperation in my speeches.”

"Uncle, we have to convince the governments of the fantastic possibilities when we act as one. My dream is that there are no more poor people, no more little crippling wars, and just one army that would help with any disasters. We could be the best in the world in many things."

"What have you done so far to promote this goal?" Mandela asked, intrigued by Siboniso's passion.

"We already have a group of eight, mainly foreign African students at Wits. We are gathering data from as many countries as possible, and it is fantastic that I am allowed to accompany you, where I can meet many people and lay contacts."

"Sib, I don't want to dampen your enthusiasm, but here are some words of advice: make sure that when you speak to people, it is your plan and not of the government of South Africa. Further, you mentioned products and minerals; I would be cautious. You know these things are mainly in foreign hands. Then you said you have started already, meaning what?"

"Thanks, Uncle, for your excellent advice," Sib nodded. "Do not worry, I am carefully avoiding the impression that this idea comes from our government. Of course, we aim to work with all African governments once we have a comprehensive plan, including our own.

"As for foreign companies and investors, they should be happy to cooperate with the governments and share their profits. Peace and cooperation will mean no more rebels and violence, saving them much money.

"So far, we have been building relationships with people who are thinking in the same direction. Mozes was the first one, and he is diligently working on the finance side of things. We have eight black and white students from other African countries. Then, as I said, we are compiling as much information about their countries and others as possible, such as who is in charge and what makes them tick.

"Of course, while I try to make contacts when accompanying you, I never act under your name or for South Africa. The information we gather does not come from your office but mainly from the internet and talking to people.

"Oh, and the invitation to the function I attended, it was from an interesting person I met on the flight to Addis Ababa. His name is Imari; his father is an Indian businessman, and his mum is of mixed race. They live in Cape Town, where he was born. His education was in the UK, from boarding school to university. He is a mining engineer and consultant with a business degree as well. I am going to get him in."

By now, Sib was quite breathless and keen to hear Mandela's thoughts.

"Sib, your goal is great, but please be prepared for many disappointments. As you must know, the Organisation for African Unity has been trying to do the same thing for many years. It is not easy to achieve cooperation. Don't forget, Africa is mainly tropical with bush and deserts and many different tribes, not to mention the Arabs in the north. Most countries have different colonial pasts, and several dictators are in power who will never agree with your plans."

"I know, Uncle, it will be difficult. The OAU has not achieved much so far. Yet, the good thing is that their offices are in Addis Ababa, and that may be a good starting point."

"I see what you mean," Mandela winked. "A young man in love often has business to do in Addis Ababa … but don't forget your other commitments."

Sib laughed. "Not to worry, Madiba, to assist you is a privilege, even if I unexpectedly have to fly to Addis Ababa."

For the rest of their flight, Mandela had a lot of other work on his hands, and Sib started writing a letter to his Makeda.

Chapter Twelve

Before they knew it was time for the national elections, which the ANC won. Nearly automatically, Nelson Mandela became South Africa's President in 1994. People were dancing in the streets; a sense of optimism swept the country. The end of apartheid would be celebrated every year from now on, with a national holiday called Freedom Day on April 27.

Being president though, in what had been a white-ruled country with many racist behaviours, was to bring diverse challenges and required many changes. The ANC had to share power with the National party and the Inkatha party, which worked because of Mandela's diplomatic skills and the prevailing goodwill. It would take quite some time before Mandela and his staff had the opportunity to visit other countries again.

———— + ————

Imari called earlier than expected to let Sib know he was in town. He invited Sib for dinner that same evening.

"I would love to," Sib said, "but what are you doing this afternoon? If you could make time, I would like to introduce you to my friends."

"The big man himself?" Imari questioned.

"No, that isn't likely. I want to show you around and have my friends meet you."

"Okay. Pick me up at my hotel at three o'clock."

Imari was waiting for him and soon, they were back at Sib's office, where he proudly pointed to the old copper nameplate in the hall of the just-elected president.

Mozes got up from his desk to shake Imari's hand and then conferred Frank's apologies for being unable to be there until much later. The three of them went to a private corner in their regular café spot next door to talk. Imari was interested when they told him about their ambitious plans; he even got enthusiastic.

Siboniso said to him, "I hope you don't mind that I researched your credentials through the university channels. I am impressed! We feel fortunate and happy to have you as a friend and a member of our group, if you want to."

"Well, I am impressed with your idea. It is something we can put our teeth in, a great and worthy plan. I am in!"

Sib asked if it was alright to bring his two friends to dinner that night. "We can split the bill."

"No! Nonsense," Imari responded. "It all goes on the expense account. But tell me more about your friend Frank; you said he is American?"

"Yes, he is a computer programmer at the American Consulate. However, he also has Nigerian nationality, although he looks more American than African."

"Hmm, I am naturally suspicious of Americans connected to their government. How much does Frank know about your plans?" "Not very much, why?"

"Guys, this idea of yours could become big. I thank you for your trust and would like to participate. But I want to be sure that the people joining us do that for the right reasons. I have worked with big businesses and met high-flyers who only think of their national interests and others who are manipulators in international politics to benefit their wealth or power.

"So, I suggest that, yes, of course, let Frank join us tonight, but let me suss him out before we reveal much about your fantastic idea. There are other things to talk about. Maybe we can talk about our trip to Addis Ababa?"

"Yes," agreed Sib. "We certainly can!" Then and there, he made up his mind to tell Mozes and Frank about Makeda and how Imari had helped to give them time alone.

The dinner went well, the food was great, and they enjoyed each other's company. Imari got Frank to talk about his life and dreams. They heard that he knew much about the continent of Africa and had been to Nigeria to visit his grandparents and several other countries to help set up their internet. Frank loved the African vibe, the music, nature, and the wildlife.

When Frank went to the bar to buy them another drink, Imari told Sib and Mozes that he was much reassured. He agreed that Frank could be a great asset to their team.

Soon after, they told Frank about their plan of African unity.

At first, their new friend needed clarification about the chances of such a plan succeeding. However, after hearing about the contacts they already had and the research they were doing, he became enthusiastic. Siboniso was delighted. In his mind, 'the top team' of their group was complete.

Mozes had many computer questions for the American. Frank laughed and said, "Slow down, Mozes. Let's set a date, then I'll come to your office and check out your computers. I can improve your internet access and help you understand the technology."

Imari boasted that he was the Cupid who had introduced Sib to the love of his life. Of course, Mozes and Frank wanted to know more, teasing him good heartedly and wanting invitations to the wedding. Sib laughed and said it would be a long-distance love affair until he improved his finances.

When they prepared to leave, Mozes declared, "Man, now our country is abolishing apartheid. I want to eat here at least once a week. It was fantastic. Thank you, Imari!"

"Well, Mozes, you will be our treasurer, so you can take us out weekly."

"That's a good idea! As soon as you start paying for your membership; we must discuss that!"

Before leaving, they set a date for their first formal meeting at Sib and Mozes's office to establish their group's rules. Frank agreed that he would try to answer all their internet and computer questions afterwards.

Frank returned to his hotel while Imari gave Sib and Mozes a lift home. In the car, Imari started talking about Frank again. He said he was likeable and that having a computer whizz on their team would be helpful.

"I feel that we can trust his good intentions," announced Imari, "but he is still an employee of the US Government. He needs to swear to keep our plans secret. Once we go public, he must quit his job and work full-time with us, as we must all do to succeed in our endeavours."

Imari warned them to be wary of sharing information about how to deal with mine and oil companies in Africa until Frank had fully committed.

"Thanks, my friends," he added. "Let's proceed cautiously. I'll be away until just before our planned meeting. Stay safe!" With these words, Imari waved goodbye.

Siboniso was mightily pleased when, during his graduation ceremony, he received an award for finishing his master's degree as the top international law student. It was even more of an occasion to celebrate as President Mandela was the guest of honour and handed him the award. That part of the ceremony and Mandela's speech were filmed and shown on TV in real-time. His parents were watching, and he knew they would be very proud.

Nelson Mandela, having been a law graduate from the same university, congratulated Siboniso and all the other students. In his speech, he shared experiences from his student years. There were funny stories but also sad ones about several encounters with the security police cracking down on activist student groups. "For the future of the Republic of South Africa, it is most important that the judiciary stays independent and impartial without blame, or hate, or favouritism."

Mandela further emphasised that otherwise, a safe and prosperous South Africa would never be.

"The law will deal with past and future crimes, and

although we must never forget, we need to forgive. I know it will not be easy, but it is the only way forward."

Mandela received much positive feedback about his talk from the legal fraternity and the general public. It was the confirmation he and others needed that he was on the right path.

Chapter Thirteen

President Nelson Mandela, a great supporter of the planned change of the OAU into a new organisation, sometimes sent Siboniso to the head office in Addis Ababa with confidential reports. South Africa's great warrior of peace was frequently involved in peace negotiations between states or rival tribes.

Siboniso could not have been happier with these instructions, as it allowed him to see Makeda.

Of course, her brother Aman accompanied them when they had dinner in one of the best restaurants. Aman was sympathetic to their love and left them alone for brief moments. They could only hold hands and reconfirm their promises, but it was enough for Siboniso to 'walk on air' for the rest of his time in the capital of Ethiopia.

Sib also met with the few contacts his group had established in that country. One was also a delegate from the Ethiopian Government to the Organisation of African Unity. He said that the OAU could soon invite them to present their case. He thought that their combined efforts might benefit the growth towards a united Africa. But he also warned that many delegates had been there from the start and were reluctant to change.

Slowly, new, younger and progressive people joined the delegations to the OAU, but the older and more conservative representatives were still too powerful. They would not consider giving up any piece of their country's independence.

Siboniso agreed that they had to be patient. He assured the member of the OAU that they were not trying to interfere with any country's autonomy. Their goals were similar, and both sought ways to work together toward a thriving continent. Siboniso confirmed that they fully supported a two-thirds majority of the total membership to endorse new laws.

After a final phone call to Makeda, Sib boarded the plane back to South Africa, dreaming of a happy future with his girl.

Mozes picked him up from the airport with the news that Frank had invited them to another party, the next day, in Cape Town. Mozes hadn't attended the previous time and was keen to go; the same jazz band and Jessie would be performing. Sib had so much on his mind that he called Frank and explained that it was all too much. But Frank talked him into going. "Hé, pal! You need to have a break sometime. I have flight and show tickets for the four of us; we will return the next morning at ten thirty."

Mozes was excited and loved every minute of the pleasant evening. Siboniso told them a bit about his experiences in Addis Ababa. He showed them a photo of Makeda that he had taken during their dinner and shared his hopes for the future.

Jessie did not have to be invited as, during the break, she joined them at their table and said it made her very happy to see them. She flirted with Siboniso, like the last time. Frank joked about Siboniso not being available, but the other three were!

Frank and Jessie then shared stories about growing up in America and compared them to Mozes' and Imari's experiences. When Jessie returned to the band, Frank said that the next party would be in Pretoria if everything worked out and that he hoped they would attend again.

One day, unexpectedly, Imari called and asked Sib to hold an extraordinary meeting for the 'top team'. Frank had to decline as the South African government department of communication asked him to urgently assist with their head office's internet access. He advised that he would join them later.

The three men decided to have dinner together at the tavern next door, catering to all races since the presidency of Mandela. There was no need to sit on the back terrace anymore. Inside, there were small, secluded corners, perfect for dinner meetings.

Upon arrival, they shared a drink before dinner while exchanging new developments since the last meeting. During dinner, Imari told them the reason for the 'extra' meeting. He got their attention when he shared his thoughts about finding money to fund their work. Mozes' attention was especially captured, as he had been breaking his head over the same thing. They couldn't continue to put their own money in, but who would fund something that most would consider a pipe dream?

"You know my profession," Imari started, "and my commitment to our cause. What you do not know is that I spent my practice year here, in the mines on the Witwatersrand. During that year, I had my eyes wide open and, too often, my mouth. Managers don't often appreciate that of a young student.

"Anyway, I worked in a small mine on the southeast side of Johannesburg and soon after I returned to the UK, the owners closed the mine. They said it was not profitable anymore, but I knew there was still lots of gold at only three to four hundred meters deep. I told them that, but they were dubious, probably wondering what would somebody studying mining in England know?

"Managers of several mines in that district convinced their owners that all gold at that level was gone. The small mine also went deeper and deeper, as far as 2 km down, until they found gold again, but at a much higher cost. As a result, they went bankrupt, and the mine had to be closed. I have had another look at my papers though, and this has convinced me that my opinion is correct. In the meantime, the price of gold is so much higher now."

Frank joined their table when the tavern's chef presented the dessert. To the chef's disappointment, they paid no attention as they eagerly informed Frank about Imari's proposal.

"I suggest we try to buy that mine," Imari urged, because our plans will cost big money."

"You can say that again," agreed Mozes, "but how can we ever afford to buy a goldmine?"

"If I am right, it'll cost a fraction of what it is worth. The mine owners have given up hope of getting a reasonable price."

"Say we find the money; then will it be safe to operate a mine that has not functioned for a while?" Mozes asked. "Also, how much money is needed for repairs, and do we need a license?"

And Frank wanted to know, "Who will run it, Imari? Are you thinking about running it yourself?"

"Yes!" exclaimed Imari. "If we agree to buy the mine, I will run it for a start. I know good people to run it later on, and I presume that Siboniso can organise a group of about sixty good miners from his home country."

"That would be the least of our problems," Sib nodded. "Our country is known for the good workers we bring to the Rand, but the money?" He looked questioningly at Mozes, who commented, "I suggest allowing Imari to investigate the condition of the mine and the circumstances. If his report is positive, we have to give it a go. Issue shares and make a deal with a bank."

Sib added, "I hope you co-board members agree that I can talk to my uncle, Madiba, about this. Let's meet again soon for progress. Imari, thanks for presenting this grand idea; it could solve our financial needs, if it works out."

<hr>

When Siboniso had a chance to talk to the President, he was very pleased he had done so. Uncle Nelson told him to get his facts together and present a decent proposal. He explained that he would not buy shares for himself but would suggest that the government buy ten per cent of the mine.

Then Mandela asked, "Does your new mine have a name?" Without even thinking, Sib said, "The Unity Mine." Adding, "If the team agrees, of course."

Chapter Fourteen

THE FIRST COUPLE OF MONTHS were hectic, with many hurdles to overcome as the men progressed their plans to buy the mine.

One of the biggest problems was that the mine could only start after the old mine was declared safe and the workers' quarters were adequate. There was a lot to do. So Siboniso had to use all his lawyer skills to convince the authorities that this was the old question of the chicken and the egg.

Firstly, they had to make the work environment as safe as possible before any production could be expected. These preparations cost time and money, but Mozes had a firm grip on things and showed his worth when he got two banks, including the one he worked for, to invest.

Another problem was that the tip area for the Unity Mine needed to be bigger for the spoils generated during production. Imari had a good solution. Much of the spoils would stay on the site: they would lower a bulldozer to refill the unproductive tunnels left by the former owners around two thousand meters deep and use only a tiny space of the above-ground tip.

Imari employed one general and three assistant mine managers he had worked with before. Sib went home briefly to report to his father about their enterprise and visit friends and family. They were so convinced by his enthusiasm that the royal family bought a substantial number of shares in the Unity Mine. Additionally, his brothers helped to organise a good workforce of sixty strong, well-trained miners. They proved to be the best crew you could wish for under the guidance of capable mine captains and managers. They got paid well and sent most of their money home.

———— ✦ ————

Slowly but surely, their trust in Imari's knowledge and everybody's hard work paid off. They found gold in the upper levels, deposited it at the bank, and started paying off some debts. They rented and renovated another part of Mr Khan's offices as most of the work was done by Sib and Mozes, whose offices and sleeping quarters were still there. A copper nameplate was added to the door, The Unity Mines Ltd.

———— ✦ ————

The mine had gotten off to such a good start that soon, it didn't need all of their time anymore, so their shared dream of achieving African unity returned to the top of their agenda. Sib also continued to assist in speech writing for President Mandela and occasionally accompanied the president on his travels.

They were the good years full of hope for a better South Africa. Additionally, Siboniso made use of every opportunity he had to visit Ethiopia. The last time, just before the new elections of 1999 in South Africa, Makeda was accompanied by her mother and Aman. Makeda wanted her mother to meet the man she was so much in love with.

Makeda's mother, Princess Desta, and Siboniso liked each other straight away. They enjoyed a delicious lunch together, full of laughter and good conversation. Mother and son left for half an hour to go shopping, leaving the two lovebirds discussing their wedding plans. Sib promised to contact her father shortly after the elections.

— ✦ —

However, just before the new elections in 1999, Siboniso had trouble concentrating on his work as his last letter to Makeda came back with 'return to sender, person unknown'. It troubled him the whole day, and as soon as he found some free time, he picked up the phone and called her number. The message he heard was: "The number you have called is not connected."

Sib was distraught and could not get any more work done. The next day, he called to say he was taking time off. He kept trying Makeda's phone number but got the same result.

Finally, Sib succeeded in getting hold of Makeda's mother. Sib's fears were realised when she revealed that she had also lost contact with her daughter, who had vanished from her rooms in the palace without a trace.

"She didn't take anything," a distraught princess revealed, saying that she and her son, Aman, were desperate to find the missing girl. Her father was on a business trip and wasn't picking up his phone.

Frank wanted to help in finding Makeda. He saw how upset Siboniso was and promised to contact somebody at the American Consulate in Addis Ababa to find out what was happening.

Three of the worst days of his life passed before Frank had

some devastating news for Sib. As far as they could find out, the story was that the young lady had been married to an old sheikh. These forced marriages still went on, even though the custom was officially banned. It was probably a deal between her father and the sheikh for political or financial reasons. All her previous connections had been cut off.

Siboniso felt as if the meaning of his life had ended.

Uncle Mandela called Sib to ask what was happening. His secretary, Zelda, told the boss that his nephew didn't seem like himself when she had talked to him on the phone. Siboniso did not cry but was not far off when he told Madiba the horrible news.

When Sib contacted Makeda's mother, she confirmed that her husband had kidnapped Makeda and sold her. She vowed to find her daughter and keep Sib informed.

There was not much anybody could do or say about the situation. Platitudes like 'keep your head high', 'try to concentrate on the big goal', and 'time will heal' made no impact. Sib knew that he had to work through it himself, but feeling supported by friends and colleagues helped. Slowly, Sib got going again, putting his sadness behind him.

—— ✦ ——

More delegates to the OAU became interested in being a part of a unified Africa. On one occasion, a Christian teacher argued that he was all for unity, if the Christian faith would be taught in every school as a mandatory subject. Sib answered that colonial powers manipulated religions if it suited them, and it was often the cause of wars and division in Africa.

"Dear Father Ambrosio," Siboniso began diplomatically. "Let me quote one of the best-known African leaders, Jomo Kenyatta: 'When the missionaries arrived in Africa, they taught us to pray with closed eyes. When we opened our eyes, they had the land, and we had the Bible.'

"Religion can divide people; dictators use it to set people up against each other. People need to eat first and have opportunities to build a decent life and access education without war or a system of apartheid. When we have achieved that, people can feel free to attend any church, mosque, or other faith they choose."

— ✦ —

Such conversations were becoming a daily business. Whether one talked to a communist, socialist, capitalist, or religious leader, each was convinced that their ideas were correct, which was hard to change. Siboniso soon concluded that he did not have to change their ideas, he only had to convince them what a great continent Africa could be. It would be so much better for everybody if they combined the best ideas from each system and compromised on others.

Chapter Fifteen

MANY CONGRESSES AND international meetings were organised. One was to be held in Pretoria, where the four of them booked into a hotel.

Siboniso tried to concentrate on the opportunity and forget about his problems. However, when Frank called and said that Jessie was in town and he was organising tickets, it all came back up.

"Sorry," Sib said, "I'm too busy."

That evening, he had dinner with some clients and a glass of something too many, which might account for what happened afterwards.

Arriving back at his hotel room, he couldn't believe his eyes. Jessie was waiting for him in a sexy evening dress, relaxing on the couch as if she belonged there. "What the heck are you doing here?"

"Come to keep you a bit of company; I have missed you and have not seen you for such a long time."

While speaking, she let her dress fall open, showing a long leg.

"Offering sex as well," he spat at her.

Not picking up on his mood, Jessie said, "Love to have sex with you, sure!"

"Listen, Jessie, I'll give you a choice. I am going to the bathroom, and when I return, I'll find you gone or naked." With that, he left.

When Sib came back into the room, both were naked, and Sib commanded: "Turn around."

She did turn around, looking back over her shoulder, asking, "What are you doing, Sib? What are you doing to me?!"

"I'm just putting a condom on so I can have sex without consequences. I don't want to run the risk of being accused of something later." He then bent her forwards over the table and penetrated her 'that way'.

Jessie screamed. "Stop it, Sib! You are hurting me."

But Sib was like a man possessed. "You wanted sex," he growled. "Now, you'll get it! This is how I watched animals do it from when I was five years old, guarding my father's goats, and that's all you mean to me."

When he was finished, Jessie was in tears.

Coldly, he declared, "I am going to take a shower. You'd better be gone when I return, or I'll call security."

She was gone, but there was a note on the table: "I will only sing sad songs from now on."

His actions on that night and his behaviour troubled Sib for the rest of his life.

"No," he told himself out loud. "I cannot use the loss of my greatest love or drinking too much as excuses." He was a lawyer; he was royalty; he could not forgive himself!

But his hurt was too deep, and it was difficult to change. Soon he was rigid and bitter towards all women and had trouble working with them.

That finally changed after he went home to his parents for a few days and had a serious discussion with his mother, Queen Mantfombi. He even broke down in tears and asked her if he was doomed by his Zulu-ness that doesn't see females as equals.

His mother was sad to hear his story and to see her stepson so troubled. She smiled reassuringly and told him that was not the case. "Times have changed for Zulus. Even at school, the kids are being taught that all people are equal and deserving of respect."

The two of them reminisced about when Sib, as a kid, refused to follow orders from his mum because she was a woman.

Siboniso felt much better after that and understood that only he could change his attitude toward women. Behaving like an anti-feminist did not sit well with his profession as a lawyer, nor with his ambitious plans for Africa. So, something had to change.

First, he had to learn to live with his sadness of losing Makeda and then, he had to accept that he could not always understand females. *Their actions could be more logical*, he thought. But he didn't want to find any more excuses, and he determined that he could learn how to behave in female company.

———— ✦ ————

Everyone was sad when it was revealed that President Nelson Mandela had decided not to stand for a second term. Siboniso was worried about the future of a democratic South Africa, but he recognised that the years in the highest office had taken their toll on Mandela's health. He couldn't be expected to do another four years.

Even considering that the ANC would win, Siboniso and his friends knew they would never find another person of his stature for president.

The people of South Africa elected Thabo Mbeki in 1999.

After the change of president was announced, Mr Mandela asked Sib to continue to assist in speech writing and to accompany him on some of his travels. His engagement agenda was still full of invitations that involved unavoidable speeches.

It was, therefore, still a busy time with several overseas trips until failing health caught up with the former president, leading first to retirement before his death in 2013 at the age of ninety-five.

In the meantime, Siboniso and his team's plan for an improved United Africa was gathering support. At least fourteen countries were committed to or seriously considering their involvement. Still, that was hardly a third of what the top team wanted.

Too many countries had troubles of their own and they claimed that they had no time to spend on future dreams.

Others argued that they already belonged to the African Union, the successor of the OAU, and did not see the necessity of joining a new organisation. The team of four started to realise that it would be more realistic for their group to apply for guest status at the African Union meetings. They should not be affiliated with any country but solely focused on finding ways to solve problems between countries and organisations. Further, they needed to reconcile different opinions, to mediate between groups and to promote peace and reconciliation, so as to follow in Mandela's footsteps.

The four applied to present their case and were invited to the first official congress of the AU in Durban in 2002. About sixteen hundred delegates from the fifty-five member states attended.

Siboniso gave one of his best speeches. Firstly, he pointed out the excellent work the AU was doing and the progress that had been made over the years. He assured them that the organisation would only become stronger with the additional focus their team would bring. This focus was aimed at improving life conditions and safety for the ordinary African person so all inhabitants of the continent would feel connected. He sketched the big dream, where one's problem was everybody's problem and together, they would find solutions.

"It is not expected that the rich pay for the poor, although fair taxes are, of course, necessary," he explained. "No, we will find ways to help those poorer districts to get self-sufficient. Each area has something favourable, be it arts, tourism, or minerals, so, with help and encouragement, it is intended that they will soon be able to look after themselves and contribute as a part of the total. "Investments in factories or anything else required, such as a dam, a canal, and connecting roads; these will all provide work opportunities for people. Then, people can buy food for their family and send their kids to be educated."

Siboniso's impassioned speech was received with some mixed reactions, so he continued. He hoped to drive in his points further. "I know some think this idea is going to cost too much money! In the start-up, maybe, but it will pay for itself in the long run. If we coordinate to sell our products globally, we can pay decent salaries and, if necessary, attract brains from overseas.

"One thing we must emphasise and impress on our citizens is that we all are Africans. Let us be one! And learn from the hard lessons of the past."

Siboniso's passion for their cause caught the imagination of many delegates. The AU invited the team to attend the yearly meetings as observers while developing a more detailed plan for integrating their ideas into the organisation. To become a permanent subgroup of the AU, they were advised that they would need the direct support of more than half of the African governments.

One of the members of Sib's growing support group had organised a meeting with the military commander of his country. Sib accepted, knowing that the man was a bully. The commander started to torpedo anything Sib might use to promote African unity before Sib said a word. Sib had seen this tactic before. He was a lawyer after all. He did not argue with the general or present any plan but quietly sat listening to many negative comments on peace and reconciliation. Finally, the general ran out of steam and sitting back with crossed arms, he waited for Sib's reaction.

"Thank you, General," Sib started. "Allow me to respond with a question. In your opinion, which is the wealthiest nation in the world?"

"The United States, of course."

"And how much bigger is the US in comparison with Africa?"

"A couple of times, I think."

"General, Africa is four times bigger than the US, and we have about a billion more people; think about that. You have heard rumours about a United African Army. If that happens in the future, we need good soldiers with experienced and knowledgeable officers and sufficient funds to attract those people. To whom can I better explain this than to a professional soldier?"

Leaning forward, Sib continued. "What if we had a defence force that was a defence force that never intended to invade other territories? It would be a different kind of army. And it would cost a lot less. Please think about those things: strong leaders for the big stuff, not the boss over a tiny part. Okay, your country has not got oil or gold like some others. Still, if I am correct, you have some minerals that are even more important in the technological world today."

Sib paused for effect. "With the proper infrastructure, exploration can become profitable for your country and the environment. Please think it through. Nobody expects you to turn around immediately, but we would love your country's support.

"Take your time and share your ideas about the role you could play in a new army. In planning for the future, we will need expertise like yours."

Chapter Sixteen

ON A SUNNY MORNING in the spring of 2004, Siboniso received a telegram. It came from Ethiopia, stating: "Arrive at 15:10 at Jo'burg International Airport, M."

Sib's first thought was, *Makeda*! But then he dismissed it. *It couldn't be, not after five years*!

The whole day, his head kept telling him it wouldn't be her, but his heart kept hoping. So, he went.

He could not believe his eyes when *his* Makeda came through the gate. Sib opened his arms, and she ran into them. For a while, they could not speak a word.

The first thing he said: "Coffee or a taxi?"

"Hello to you too," she smiled. "Coffee, please."

They went to the lounge and then just let their coffee get cold while Makeda told her story.

"The sheikh had a massive heart attack, and, in the confusion, I took the kitchen money and paid the taxi driver, who had just delivered a doctor, to take me to the airport," she revealed breathlessly.

"Thank heavens you escaped!" exclaimed Sib, holding her hands in his. "Today is the best day of my life. I have missed you so much! But tell me everything. Was there enough money to buy a ticket?"

"At the airport, I called my mother, who raced to meet me.

We were so happy to see each other again. She had no idea where I was imprisoned or even if I was still alive. She brought proof of my identity, paid for the ticket, and I sent you the telegram. We had lunch while waiting for departure.

"My mum cried when she saw me. We both did and we couldn't talk for a while." Tears ran down Makeda's face as she remembered this, and she bit her lip to continue. "Then Mama started telling me what happened after I went missing. My father told her and my brother that he had sold me into marriage and refused to disclose where to find me. She was furious and called the guards to escort him out. She told him not to come near her again unless he brought me home. Aman wanted nothing to do with him, either. When their divorce went through, my father went into such a rage that he got a powerful stroke. He now needs twenty-four hours' care in a special home."

In a low, emotional voice, Makeda continued. "They tricked me, Sib, darling. Without telling me anything, three strong men forcefully shoved me into a car and blindfolded me. I screamed and fought, but they put a cloth in my mouth and held me down. After a short drive, they allowed me to get out and look around, but all I could see was the courtyard of a vast, heavily guarded palace.

"I have lived in luxury in the women's quarters. But for all these years, the only outside I have seen has been the court-yard. "Because of my education, I had to teach the twelve children of the other three wives. I was the fourth one.

"I never got the chance to get out or even send you a message, my love. His first wife was a dragon, making life difficult for us, but I got along well with the other two wives, locked up like I was. "However, all I wanted was to escape, and I tried several times, but the guards caught me every time."

"I thought I would never see you again," Sib replied, hugging her tightly. "But I never wanted to date another girl; I hope you will believe that. I kept in contact with your mother and Aman. We employed a private detective who got nowhere. He tried several times to talk to your father, who, as you know now, has lost the ability to communicate. However, he must have understood something as he got very agitated. Afterwards, they refused the detective further visits.

"Because of the divorce, your mother had no access to her former husband's papers or phone, and neither had the detective.

"Then, this year, I tried for the first time to accept that I would never see you again and attempted to ban you from my thoughts. But I couldn't do it!" Sib held tightly to Makeda's hand. "You were and always will be the only one. Oh, Makeda, it took so long!"

Not sure how to talk about sleeping arrangements with Makeda, Siboniso ordered a separate room for her. Awkwardly, he kissed her good night and went to his room. Lying awake, he worried how to approach the subject.

The following day, it was early when Sib knocked on Makeda's door and asked if she would like breakfast in bed or downstairs in the dining room.

"Downstairs," Makeda replied. "Please give me twenty minutes."

When seated, there was tension between them, and finally, Makeda could wait no longer.

"Why didn't you want to sleep with me?"

Sib could see that she had not slept well either and sheepishly, he replied, "I thought you might want to wait until we were properly married. We never had a chance to talk about this, and I didn't want to push you."

"What a lame excuse, Siboniso," scoffed Makeda. "Is it because I was married before? If so, I have a surprise for you. The old man has damaged nothing in my body. There was no wedding ceremony, and the other wives told me he hadn't touched them in a long time. Having a fourth wife was just a prestige thing. I was a slave teacher."

Many emotions fought for attention in Siboniso; he had trouble finding words. He felt guilty thinking of her in the old sheikh's arms, enormous gratitude that she would be all his and regret that he had allowed his confused feelings to interfere with their first night together.

Jumping up, he left his seat and went to hug her tightly. "Forgive me, Makeda, please! I love you so much; I will make it up to you."

"It's okay," Makeda smiled, hugging him back. "I love you, too. I am so sorry this has happened to us. We may need some time to work through the experiences of the last five years. I was afraid to find you happily married to somebody else!"

There was no more time for privacy, as Nelson Mandela had only made an hour available for the young couple. His congratulations were so enthusiastic that he even danced and got them to dance with him. He was so pleased for them. Together, they sat down for refreshments while meeting Mandela's third wife, Graça, for the first time in an informal way. Their outward demeanour showed them that this marriage made them both happy and content. Sib was delighted. He felt it was a well-deserved base for the last period of the former president's life.

— ✦ —

After this visit, Siboniso had some appointments that he could not cancel. It became a long and tedious day for him, but Makeda relished her freedom. She happily shopped in town for essentials and returned to the hotel for long phone conversations with her mother and Aman.

— ✦ —

Siboniso managed to take a week off for a pre-marriage honeymoon at a small hotel in the Drakensberg Mountains, southeast of Johannesburg. The couple needed that time to get to know each other anew.

Even though they were sure of their love, they had only met each other occasionally during their courtship. Even then, they had hardly been left alone. Apart from exchanging many letters and having phone conversations, a total silence of five years had then followed when Makeda had been kidnapped.

It was a wonder, therefore, that they both had still kept dreaming about a future life together. They shared those dreams during long walks through the mountains. Both were hesitant about showing their sexual hunger for each other, afraid of upsetting the other, but it wasn't long before their desire took over, and they knew they were made for each other.

Their happiness radiated from them when they visited Siboniso's family. Sib proudly presented Makeda as his future wife to his parents. She was received with open arms, and Siboniso's oldest brother immediately started planning for a three-day wedding in Nongoma.

Meeting Sib's extended family was quite an experience for Makeda. Her warm personality made it easy for her new in-laws to welcome and love her. Siboniso proudly showed her the places of his youth, like where he had shepherded with his cousins and the mission school he had attended for his early schooling. During a welcome party for Makeda, he got the chance to introduce her to some of the friends and cousins he grew up with.

Makeda recognised some of the royal traditions as similar to the ones in her country, but was happy that her father didn't have six wives. Before they returned to their Drakensberg hotel, the family came together and agreed to a three-day wedding in late 2005, after an already planned trip of Siboniso around Africa.

Chapter Seventeen

After a few more relaxing days, it was back to reality and a full agenda for Sib. During their holiday, the couple had discussed where they would like to settle. Makeda was charmed by the city of Pretoria especially how, annually, it was festooned with purple blossoming jacaranda trees. She had visited the capital of South Africa with her family just before she met Sib, and it reminded her of happier times.

So, Makeda went house hunting while Sib returned to his many responsibilities: speaking tours with Mandela, doing some work for his old boss Manish Khan, meetings about the Unity Mine, and planning his African trip, all based in Johannesburg. It left little time to join Makeda, who managed to find a lovely house on the outskirts of Pretoria on a street lined with jacarandas.

Her mother came over to help her furnish it and find some personnel. Princess Makeda had a bank account, which her wealthy mother funded. Sib joined them whenever he could.

The plan was that, before the wedding, Siboniso would undertake an intensive but quick tour around Africa, visiting as many countries as possible. After much research and phone calls, Mozes made appointments with decision-makers in countries that fitted into a round trip from south to north, via the west, and back via the east coast. Sib promised his love that he would try to do it in a few weeks. Even for a strong young man, this promised to be an extremely tiresome trip. And it was. Things could have been better organised in some countries, and time was lost by just waiting around. Then, the weather interfered, causing delayed flights and missed appointments. Sometimes, the appointment with one person was changed to a speaking opportunity some days later at a sitting of that country's government.

Sib could not let such an opportunity go, although the ministers would bombard him with questions that he couldn't always answer. It afforded him a good exercise in diplomacy. He then assured them that he had taken note, would consult with his team, and come back later. Another consequence of the delays was that he had to contact Mozes to reschedule the subsequent meetings. One of the most asked questions was, "Do you envision a system like the United Nations, with a security council with veto rights for some countries?"

"A security council maybe," Sib would always reply, "but countries with a veto, never. We have seen in practice how that hampers good decisions. As a model for the future, it's better to look at the United States, but also at the European Union. We want to learn from both systems but only implement appropriate policies for our continent."

"Will we be getting one currency for the whole of Africa?"

"That is a possibility and could be a good thing, but again, we need to thoroughly discuss proposals like that before a majority vote decides on them."

"You are a member of the ANC, and they are said to be of the far left. Is that the direction you want all members to go?"

"I am glad you asked that question because I had no idea people were wondering about that. Firstly, I am not a member of the ANC, strange as that may sound, as I greatly admire my uncle, Nelson Mandela. I have never been a member.

"Secondly, the political direction of the African Union, as it is or as it might become, is totally up to the members of that organisation. An organisation promoting a unified Africa shouldn't be a political organisation, in my view. Instead, I think it should be a unifying tool for all nations of any persuasion.

"By the way, the ANC is leaning toward social democracy. It's not as far left as you might think. I hope that answers your question."

⸻ ✦ ⸻

Before going to the northeast countries, an exhausted Sib had to rest for a few days. When his plane landed at Dakar, he booked into a luxury resort for three days and called Mozes to delay all of his appointments, as he needed to recharge.

Remembering Aunt Magogo teaching him how to recover from extreme tiredness, Sib took the time to follow her advice to meditate daily and felt his brain and body heal. Between swimming and resting his body, he wrote reports of his visits and sent them to the team.

Of course, there were long phone conversations with Makeda, every day. She was very interested in everything he and his team worked for, and talking with her made him feel they were on the right path. She also told him how much fun she and her mum had preparing the house for his return.

"Don't worry about anything," she said, "and make sure you are rested before you start your trip again. I love you, and everything else can wait till you're home."

—— ✦ ——

Sib also studied the rest of his travel plan, noticing that the island of Madagascar was missing, which disturbed him a bit. The more he read about the island, the more he knew they needed support from the African Union. He contacted Mozes and got his assurances that he would organise a visa for him in the Kenyan embassy and a plane ticket to the island.

Refreshed, Sib started the new list of appointments in the northern countries. It was hectic, but by now, Sib was more experienced and better able to deal with bureaucrats, ministers and sometimes the country's president or another leader.

Often, he looked back with nostalgia at the times he had accompanied President Mandela. Those times, they were welcomed everywhere with enthusiasm and respect. Of course, he could never attain that same level of respect, but he could strive for understanding and cooperation in the spirit of the esteemed African leader. Being a former aide to Mandela certainly helped to open doors.

Although Siboniso was happy with the reactions he received in several countries, they were mainly countries with more or less democratically elected governments. If not, they at least tried to improve their citizen's circumstances by looking after infrastructure and services.

However, there were at least as many countries where his

appointments had no results, leaving him deflated and disappointed. These countries were the least developed, with poor services and a lot of civil unrest. The government officials he met were often fatalistic about it and mostly looked after themselves and their families first, rather than after their citizens.

Sib knew that it was those countries that needed the African Union the most and would benefit by becoming an active member. However, the response was lacklustre when Sib argued his case at their meetings. He got nowhere and, in the end, he decided to leave it for another visit in the future after consulting with his team.

Chapter Eighteen

Checking in at the last stop in the north, the hotel receptionist handed him an invitation to a private meeting with the president of that country.

When Siboniso arrived, he had to wait a bit because the room had to be de-bugged. When they finally sat down, they politely chatted about the country, its beauty and the existing industries before getting to the reason for Siboniso's visit. The President was aware that Siboniso's group was advocating a new direction for the African Union. He wanted to know Siboniso's thoughts about the political direction of a changed African Union.

"Mr President, thank you for allowing me to make our case. The question about politics is complicated. Believe it or not, despite finishing a law degree at the Witwatersrand University in Johannesburg and experiencing the apartheid regime, I have never wanted to get involved in politics.

"I am interested in justice and like to leave politics to others. I am sorry, but I can't give you a fitting answer. So far, we have mainly concentrated on the ideal of a great united Africa, and we trust that leaders from countries that wish to join us have that ideal as a priority and agree on direction later."

"Mr Siboniso, I now have a tricky question. I am talking openly. We have oil for which foreign companies have set up the infrastructure. They then pump oil from our earth, our soil. The government gets paid in agreed royalties. Outside that, I also get something for every barrel. What are your plans in this direction?" "Thank you, your Excellency, for being open with me. As you have said, this is a tricky question. Please remember that nothing has been agreed on yet."

"I am just asking for your vision, Siboniso. Your team must have considered this, as many countries are in the same situation."

"My vision and I think my team's vision is that the oil from your country, the oil from other African countries, and the gold, and diamonds, and cobalt, and all minerals from Africa, are from Africa. So, if anybody else wants it, they might have to bargain with a country for exploration rights with strict rules about rights and duties. The country's government should have joint ownership and employment rights. Africa as a whole should have a common export market, setting prices and sharing profits.

"Please know that this vision is flexible."

As the President regarded him with penetrating eyes, Siboniso added, "We welcome discussion and new ideas. Our advice to all countries that depend on foreign investments is to try educating and training your people for employment in the existing and new industries. Be prepared."

"I think I see what you mean," the President answered slowly. "What do you expect from countries that still closely connect with the old colonial powers?"

"Let us hope that, while keeping friendly relations, they

will learn to look after their own country and do not need them anymore.

"One more thing, Mr President, in the short time I have been travelling through this northern part of Africa, I have seen the problems with immigrants or refugees. People have told me that many people drown as they take significant risks to find a better life. I have also heard about rebels and terrorists making countries unsafe. I believe that they are often financed by foreign dictatorships, encouraging religious fanaticism.

"Imagine having one Africa, with factories, industries, agriculture and tourism, providing plenty of paid work. If people had a roof above their heads, peace in their country, and work to provide food and education, would that not solve these problems?" "Interesting, Siboniso. Probably not in my time, but it's worth working for in the long run. It seems a desirable solution."

— ✦ —

Hoping to find some support in one of the poorest countries, Siboniso pushed on with his plan to visit Madagascar.

Mozes told Sib to go to the Madagascar Consulate in Nairobi to organise a visa. The Consul expected Siboniso and had contacted his government after receiving a letter from Sib's team. They appreciated his visit, and one of their ministers would be available to welcome him. It sounded well planned, but the reality needed to meet expectations.

After a three-hour flight to the island, Sib arrived at their main airport. The airport emigration authorities were unprepared for his arrival and took their time. Finally, after waiting a few hours, a government car arrived with just the driver to transport him to his hotel, as it had become too late for an appointment. The main road to the capital's centre was blocked for unknown reasons.

The driver said, "If you don't mind, Sir, I know the back roads to the centre and will deliver you safely to your hotel. The minister has time for you after 10 am tomorrow. I will pick you up just before that."

Siboniso readily agreed. He was looking forward to a rest after the long day. The drive took them through some terrible slums. Only someone familiar with the condition of the roads could have made it safely.

Many houses were dilapidated whereas others were just tents or cardboard fabrications. While driving through here, the government car drew attention in the crowded areas. Some people extended their hands to beg, while others raised their fists. Siboniso felt uncomfortable, but the driver seemed unperturbed.

Stopping at a petrol station when the surroundings improved, the driver said, "I hope you don't mind this short stop. I live not far from here. If I fill up the car at this station, I get a big discount for my car's petrol."

While at the station, some youngsters came to the limousine trying to sell porno magazines. They were chased away but were followed by others, offering cocaine or even more potent drugs. These actions made Sib quite depressed. He was relieved when they went on their way after the driver had shooed them away.

At meetings the next day, Sib received the response he had heard before. "We are too poor to have time for that!"

Sib's answer was also the same. "I have seen that you have big problems, which means you could benefit from association with our team that's aiming to improve the effectiveness of the AU. It's only in cooperation that we will improve Afric a's future."

But once again, his message of hope fell on deaf ears. Sib knew that they needed it so much, but he felt this extra trip had been a waste of time.

— + —

Back home, the first one to welcome him at the airport was Makeda. They hugged, and both vowed to avoid such an extended separation again.

They would propose that Makeda would become a full partner in the team and accompany her husband on future travels. There was no problem when Siboniso told his team. They all agreed they could use a woman's perspective on their team.

Chapter Nineteen

Before travelling on to Pretoria, Siboniso and Makeda sat down with Mozes, Imari and Frank and analysed Siboniso's travel results.

Only five more countries had pledged support for their future aims for Africa. A few more were interested but, for the time being, they just wanted to stay informed.

Sib was disappointed and blamed himself for not getting countries with the most needs on board or even thinking about it. The others didn't agree at all; they thought he had done a splendid job. They emphasised the significant achievement that Siboniso had shared the ideas of their group with all countries, including the ones that were most troubled and less responsive. They all agreed it would make the next step easier.

"This is a long-term project, Sib. We are talking about fifty-five countries, and we already have more than fourteen in a reasonably short time. Your trip has added five more."

The countries most resistant to joining seemed to be the ones in the north of Africa. Not that there were more poor people in their countries than in other countries; it was more a matter of trust. That was the hardest to achieve; deep down, it was a form of racism, but Siboniso and his team vowed never to give up.

The team had experienced discrimination, racism and apartheid, whatever you want to call it, based on colour, religion, or nationality all their lives, and they had gotten past that. It was possible; they knew that they just had to keep at it.

———— ✦ ————

They talked about the time when rebels seized power on one of the Comoros Islands, east of Mozambique. The AU had sent in its African army to free the island, resulting in the flight of the rebel leader and the disappearance of the rest without any bloodshed. It was proof that effective leadership is possible.

Another positive achievement was that, when disasters struck, the African Union worked with the United Nations and the Red Cross to provide basic needs. On the other hand, the Peace and Security Council had been less successful in mitigating other conflicts in African countries. Rebels, terrorists, and civil wars continued to spread havoc throughout the continent. They knew that there is nothing worse than a civil war where people from the same country fight against each other, often in the same village or sometimes even within the same family.

———— ✦ ————

They assured each other that they were on the right path. The AU needed to change. The basis was correct, but the organisation must become more credible and effective. They would stick with them, garner support, and reach that goal.

———— ✦ ————

Finally, Makeda and Siboniso left for Pretoria, where Makeda proudly showed off the home she had furnished and decorated with the help of Desta, her mother. She managed to create a stylish as well as a welcoming and comfortable home.

Sib was amazed when he found a large room designed as

his office and meeting room for the team. Frank had connected the office to the internet, and the separate entrance provided privacy and security. He couldn't be happier.

Very thoughtfully, Mother Desta had already left for her home in Addis Ababa. She understood they needed time together to enjoy their home and prepare for their wedding.

—— ✦ ——

During the same period, the Peace and Security Council of the AU was meeting in Pretoria. Several delegates of the AU were in town, so Siboniso managed to organise several appointments even though this was far from easy.

"Yes, it is a great vision," some agreed, but most delegates did not see how it could work.

Sib argued, "If you, in principle, support the vision, you might come to see the great possibilities. Please understand that a contribution from our team, supported by a growing number of AU member states, would only complement your work. Think about all the AU negotiations to stop fighting in several countries and the problems left by the old colonial system.

"If, together, we can uplift Africa and improve circumstances for the common people, there won't be any more need to join rebels or terrorists. We can find ways to combine all our resources to become powerful as a continent and make trade deals overseas. Sib continued to urge his counterparts for their support. "Foreign investments must be made on a fifty-fifty basis with the country they invest in. Profits can then be used to improve infrastructure, local industries and agriculture. I don't know how yet, but nothing will ever change if we don't get together, exchange ideas, and support initiative."

Sib accepted an invitation to present their view at the Peace and Security Council. Some delegates had already pledged their support for the team's vision. They helped achieve a positive platform. The feedback was promising.

Afterwards, Siboniso and Makeda travelled to Ethiopia to visit her mother and brother to discuss their wedding preparations. They also met the rest of her family and childhood friends to introduce them to Makeda's husband-to-be. Sib enjoyed meeting everybody and invited them all to the wedding in Nongoma in 2006.

Makeda also visited her father to confront him with her anger, but was shocked to find him an old, broken man with a feeble mind. He even had trouble recognising her. Her anger changed to pity, but no love remained in her heart.

Her mother, Princess Desta, distantly related to King Haile Selassie, still looked young. It was clear where Makeda got her beauty from. Desta's family was influential in this part of the world, and this helped Siboniso spread his message to people outside the AU members.

Their wedding was a big occasion that spread over three days back in Sib's hometown. The Council of Nongoma adorned the town with flags and decorations. Wedding guests booked all of the accommodation that was available. They came from many places: friends from Siboniso's study years and his lawyer practice; Imari's family from Cape Town and Frank's grandparents from Nigeria; Mozes, the only son of deceased parents, came on his own. And, of course, there were many family members and friends of Makeda who attended. They all mixed happily with Siboniso's royal family, his father's six wives and their children and grandchildren. The meeting between Princess Desta and Queen Mantfombi started a firm friendship. They both were very happy with the choice their children had made. Siboniso and Makeda did not dress in traditional wedding attire. They wanted to show their independence of any tribe and present as a modern African couple. Makeda was dressed in an off-the-shoulder long white satin dress, a white crown-like jewel adorning her shiny black hair. She looked amazing next to her proud partner in a smart black suit and white satin shirt.

The King performed the wedding ceremony in front of a small family gathering. Afterwards, they stepped outside, and all the guests and the people of Nongoma welcomed them as a couple with thundering applause. The royal family provided a street banquet for everybody. Inside several palaces, many dances, receptions, and dinners went on for three days. Sib's brothers organised it all.

Sib and his bride went from occasion to occasion, socialising with all and having the time of their lives. Still, before the three days were over, the just-married couple secretly left for their official honeymoon in the same small hotel in the Drakensberg mountains where they had first rekindled their relationship two years previously.

It took a while before Makeda and Siboniso found balance

back in their lives. Arriving home, they found that the other team members had brought all their presents and flowers and distributed them throughout the house. Mozes had the key to the office and could enter the home through there.

It was a festive homecoming, but it took days to go through everything and send 'thank you' notes, letters, and emails. The photos also arrived, adding to their after-wedding busyness and enjoyment.

However, it took only a short time before they returned to real business. This involved many meetings, sometimes at their house and others in Johannesburg, where Mozes' office was still located. Their agenda included planning trips to several countries.

Chapter Twenty

Through Frank's connections in the US, they arranged a meeting with a high-ranking officer of the Blue Helmets army. The four friends and Makeda travelled to New York to meet him in 2007.

They wanted to learn how a peace corps could work in Africa. Of course, all African countries are represented in the United Nations, and many contribute soldiers to the Blue Helmets. Could Africa, as a continent, build up a peace corps specially trained to deal with African problems? And still be part of the UN Blue Helmets, hopefully receiving opportunities for training and funding?

Yes, that could be possible, although they were informed, "You must raise your own funding."

Mozes saw the enormous expenses that would entail. The officer explained that the costs had to be shared proportionally by all members.

"That could then be our biggest problem," Mozes said.

"Not if you can show that the figure would be less than what they spend on their defence now. The problem we are encountering is getting a fair amount out of every member. Because many still keep a part of their army on or double their police force.

"Another big problem is a change in government through

an election or a coup, and the incoming government has ideas other than those of the previous one. And another thing, if it works or not, often boils down to trust between the nations."

"I agree," Siboniso nodded. "We might never get rid of all mistrust; however, it is a fact that the African Union has continued to uphold the Charter of Rights for All African People to Freedom, Equality, Justice, and Dignity, established in 1963 by the Organisation for African Unity. This constitution forms the solid ground from which we must work."

They left the meeting in an optimistic mood. The officer invited them to attend the general meeting of the United Nations as observers. Mingling with attendees from countries worldwide and the earnest discussions that occurred were unforgettable experiences for them. They also did some sightseeing and, to Mozes' delight, they sampled several of New York's restaurants.

Returning home, they knew they had months of hard work and meetings to formulate proposals and ideas ahead of them. They needed to prepare for a presentation of their goals for the next general meeting of the AU. So, the team took a week off to recharge their batteries.

Siboniso had often thought about visiting the Paul Kruger National Park, northeast of Johannesburg, and talked Makeda into going. She had always lived in a city and wasn't particularly keen to get close to wild animals. However, having time with Sib without the distractions of meetings and phone calls was too precious to refuse.

They stayed in a luxury cabin with an outside area looking out over a lake where wildlife came to drink at the end of a hot day. Every day, a guide picked them up in a bush vehicle. The guide carried a gun in case of an emergency, which made Makeda feel safer.

Even though they saw nothing but monkeys on the first day, they enjoyed watching elephants, giraffes, lions, and many other animals on subsequent days. Although Makeda's uneasiness in the bush was slowly changing into wonder and enjoyment, she preferred to sit on the back terrace with Siboniso at dusk and watch the wildlife come to drink from a safe distance.

When the guide came to pick them up for a walking tour in the area, Makeda said she would be perfectly happy to stay home for a day's rest and hear about their adventures later.

Sitting quietly on their terrace, Makeda was excited to see gazelles, called 'springboks' in Afrikaans—South Africa's national symbol—venture close to their rondavel. She loved watching them frolic around and took lots of photos.

The day before, she had gotten quite a fright when climbing out of the shared swimming pool to come across a snake about six feet long. She had dived back into the pool, calling out to Sib, who was having a beer with their guide. The two men managed to remove the snake to another area and double-checked that there were no snakes in or around the rondavel.

The first few days were very tiring. In fact, they were nearly too fatigued to enjoy the delicious dinners at day's end. After that, they became used to the routine and were fortunate to see most of the wild animals the Kruger Park had to offer.

They also visited the museum and the information centre of the park. At the end of the week, they returned home, deeply impressed with this valuable asset of their country and imbued with renewed motivation to make conservation of land and animals one of their priorities.

Both of them agreed that their trip to Kruger Park had been one of the best times of their life. Makeda's feeling that she might be pregnant increased that happiness. She didn't want to say anything to Sib until she was sure. However, she couldn't keep still any longer after the nauseating spells in the morning became noticeable.

So, one morning, she sat Sib down and asked him if he could fit a baby into his busy life.

His eyes lit up. "Really? Is it true, my love? Are we going to be parents?"

He pulled her out of her chair, hugged her and took her dancing throughout the house, singing about babies and happiness. He stopped at the spare bedroom, next to theirs, and declared it as 'the *ingane*' [baby] room.

Makeda was a healthy young woman and had an easy pregnancy. In mid-2008, guided by an experienced midwife, she gave birth to a beautiful Zulu baby boy. Sib stayed with her from the start of her labour pains, holding her hand and encouraging her to follow the midwife's instructions.

As she cried out in pain when the baby's head pushed through, both their tears turned to tears of happiness as the midwife held up this perfect male baby. He screamed his little lungs out when being cleaned before he was laid on Makeda's breast, where he quieted instantly. Siboniso and Makeda had several discussions about a name for their son. Sib said that Makeda had the same rights as he had when choosing a name.

But she disagreed and said, "You are a Zulu prince. Names can be significant for our son later, maybe also for your tribe."

Sib went through the names of his ancestors but couldn't find anything suitable, not for today's world. He had to think about the future …

Then he got it. "Remember I told you about my aunt Magogo? How she taught me about Zulu culture and history, and the importance of songs, poems and stories? I introduced you to a friend of hers, Professor Bhekizizwe Peterson, when we attended the first screening of his film, *Zulu Love Letter*. He has been such an inspiration to me; thinking about a positive future for Africa, I would like to call our son after him, Bhekizizwe kaSiboniso. The name means 'looking after nations' It couldn't be better, could it?"

"I like it," Makeda said. "We'll call him Bheki."

———— ✦ ————

Bheki was a beautiful baby and a cute toddler. He was loved by everybody and adored by his grandmother Desta, who came over as soon as she heard of the birth and stayed to help for the first few weeks.

For Bheki's first birthday, the trio visited Nongoma. They celebrated a Zulu name giving ceremony with the King to add Prince Bhekizizwe kaSiboniso officially to the royal household.

The toddler was the centre of attention wherever they went.

Sib and Makeda updated the king and queen about their work and found them supportive, as always. Sib had made it a habit to consult them before visiting any African state, as they kept in contact with leaders and other royal families all over the continent. They were able to provide valuable advice and introductions to leaders. The grandparents couldn't get enough of little Bheki and were sad to see them return to Pretoria when it was time.

———— + ————

When Bheki was about three, they visited Mandela and his third wife, Graça. They now lived in Johannesburg. Mandela hugged the boy and said he hoped that Bheki would indeed be a leader of nations, but more than that, he hoped that he would lead a happy life. They only stayed a short time as, by then, Mandela was weak and ailing. It was the last time they saw Madiba.

———— + ————

On December 10, 2013, the members of the 'top team', along with Makeda and Bheki, attended Nelson Mandela's memorial service at the FNB stadium in Johannesburg. They also paid their respects at the Pretoria Municipal buildings, where they viewed their hero's body and signed the book of condolence.

It was an emotional time.

After these official events, coming together at the office where Mandela started his life as a lawyer, was a comforting experience. Their former boss, Manish Khan, and Uncle Shenge joined them to mourn and share their memories.

Chapter Twenty-One

A CALL CAME IN FROM ONE of the AU delegates of a central African country, inviting Siboniso to a meeting with that country's president.

As they always did when preparing for an overseas trip, they informed the Department of Foreign Affairs of their plans. They got the go-ahead, but the advice was to be cautious. A rebel army had attacked several villages, randomly killing people while stealing valuables and food.

The team knew that, although several of that country's leaders were not keen on their plans for Africa, their president was interested and willing to listen. They expected others would follow if they could get this country along.

Because it would be difficult, Imari and Sib decided to go together. Imari had extensive knowledge about the mining industry in that country, which would be very useful in the discussions they expected to have.

Makeda and Bheki accompanied them to the airport, where they boarded a plane to Addis Ababa to visit Makeda's mother. Shortly after hugging them goodbye, the men boarded their flight. They had a quiet trip and were looking forward to making significant progress for their organisation.

Upon the arrival at their destination, a high-ranking officer representing the president welcomed them and led them to the waiting limousine. He informed them that the car was bullet-proof and had cost a fortune. The president was very proud of it and used nothing else.

The officer then confirmed that the country had a problem with people opposing the government. They had formed a rebel army that now also tried to recruit members in the capital, causing suspicion and mistrust. Many people hated them as they kidnapped people for ransom and plundered and terrorised their fellow citizens, so far, mostly in small, remote villages. The officer assured them that extra security had been organised for their stay.

Sitting in the back of the limousine with the officer next to the driver, the guests felt safe travelling through the capital as they saw many police and security guards around.

Then, suddenly, everything changed. Driving past a small park, a salvo of shots rang out. The unhurt driver put his foot down, and the car shot forward, but the damage was devastating. The officer was wounded but not critically. He shouted to the driver to go to the closest hospital emergency as fast as possible and called ahead to prepare them.

At the hospital, things went into overdrive. The driver called the president's office while nurses and doctors cared for the wounded. The president immediately sent several security officers to protect the guests in the hospital, but it was too late for Imari.

The hospital informed the president that Imari had died without regaining consciousness. A bullet had gone straight through his head; he had no chance. How was it possible that bullets had penetrated a supposedly bulletproof car? This would be the subject of several investigations.

Before hitting Imari, the same bullet had gone through Siboniso's throat, nearly killing him, too. Another bullet had gone through his hip and lower back. Sib had a good chance of survival as the nurses immediately administered oxygen. It was a miracle that none of his main blood vessels were damaged.

The officer in the front of the vehicle had a nasty bullet wound on the shoulder, but, fortunately, the driver was not hurt. Because of his quick action, Siboniso would live.

The two security guards who followed the limousine had driven their motorbikes straight into the park where the shots had come from. They caught one person; however, he was just a hired assassin, with no helpful information about the person who hired him. The police expressed their confidence in finding more culprits.

The president of the republic personally phoned the president of South Africa with the terrible news. He promised to leave no stone unturned to find and prosecute the terrorists who committed such an awful crime. He added that he suspected that the rebel army had organised the attack and that it had been aimed at him, not at South Africa or her people.

⸺ ✦ ⸺

After hearing the shocking news, a devastated Makeda arrived the following morning in the first available plane from Addis Ababa to be at Siboniso's side. She left Bekhi in her mother's care.

Siboniso was in a coma for two weeks. That fortnight was

the toughest time for Makeda, who hardly left his side.

While Sib was still in a coma, she managed, with the help of the Zulu king and her mother's family, to organise an air ambulance for the transfer of Sib to the best hospital in South Africa, the Groote Schuur Hospital in Cape Town.

Once there, and after an evaluation, the specialists asked for Makeda's permission to operate on his throat; they planned to insert a plastic trachea so he could start breathing by himself again.

After a successful operation, later to be followed up by plastic surgery, they assured her that there would be little to see from the outside once it had healed.

While Sib was still unconscious, Makeda continued to sit with him, talking softly, hoping to get through to him. It seemed to help as he finally woke up. Makeda hugged him with tears of relief, but Sib was still very confused. He tried to touch his throat but felt only bandages. He could not talk!

Makeda called the nurse; and doctors soon arrived. They explained, as gently as they could, that he had lost the use of his vocal cords and that the damage to his lower back was so severe that he would not be able to walk and maybe never would again. Sib immediately descended into a deep depression.

The doctors assured him and Makeda that they would do everything possible to improve his situation. But Sib first needed to heal from this operation. At the same time, the best neurologists would examine his spinal injury and their top orthopaedic surgeon, his shattered hip.

— + —

In the meantime, Makeda's mother, Desta, moved into a furnished apartment near the Groote Schuur Hospital with her grandson, Bheki.

Between times spent with Sib, Makeda got to rest in a comfortable home surrounded by love. Every day, Bheki asked to see his father, and they promised a visit as soon as the doctor approved, giving them time to prepare the little boy.

Chapter Twenty-Two

Frank and Mozes visited a few times, but with injured vocal chords, Sib had to write down his input in every conversation; he found it tiresome and frustrating. He often shut down and turned away. It was an understandable reaction from such a young, active man trying to cope with what happened.

Additionally, although he could breathe, Sib could only swallow liquid food. His vocal cords were gone, so he could not speak and never would. It seemed also very unlikely that he would ever walk again. The realisation of all this, added to living in near-constant pain, made life unbearable for Sib.

When his friends told him that they had attended Imari's funeral and expressed the team's condolences to his parents, Siboniso broke down in tears. Only Makeda could console him.

Still, the confrontation with Imari's death made him reassess his attitude. When Imari's parents came to see him, he held their hands before writing down that Imari's life and friendship would power the team to stay motivated until they reached their goal of a united Africa.

Straight after the shooting, the South African Head of Security was able to send some of their detectives to the country of the accident. They were able to examine the so-called bulletproof vehicle. The state limousine had been peppered with bullets. Most of them did not penetrate the car, as was expected from a bulletproof car. However, as some of the bullets had been steel-capped, these speared through, causing the devastating injuries.

Sadly, the country's police never located the other shooter or shared more information. The cooperation of the president's security forces was minimal.

———— + ————

As time passed, two things managed to lift Siboniso out of his depression. The first thing was little Bheki, who was now a boisterous six-year-old. During his first visit with his injured father, he had been very quiet and subdued. It was incomprehensible to him that his happy, playful dad just lay there and couldn't even talk to him or hug him.

But the clever little boy quickly learned ways of communicating and telling his dad about what he had done that day, constantly watching Sib's eyes for a response. Sib loved it and invented new ways to communicate with his eyes, face, eyebrows, hands, and arms.

Bheki also became very good at drawing to tell his stories, and Siboniso started drawing back. The three of them began to learn sign language, which became fun because of Bheki.

The second thing that helped was Siboniso's pride in Makeda. She had been on his side most of the time, and when not, she became an effective organiser for their cause.

In addition to looking after Sib, she and Mozes answered all calls from African and overseas well-wishers. There had been many who asked for updates on the plans that Siboniso and his team had been working on for so long and so hard.

It was truly convenient that Makeda was fluent in many languages, as people appreciated being addressed in their language. The team now had monthly bedside meetings, which kept Siboniso's brain occupied with ongoing plans for African unity instead of focusing on his limitations.

Further medical interventions had succeeded in getting some movements back in his legs, but Siboniso still did not have the power to stand. The best result of his neurological treatment was that the pain was gone. The specialist said he could do nothing else for him at that stage. However, he assured him that there was much research into spinal surgery worldwide.

"Don't lose hope," he encouraged Sib. "We will keep in touch." For now, they planned for his return to their house in Pretoria. He would get ongoing physiotherapy and regular tests to monitor further healing of his body.

The day came, three months after the attack, that the medical staff at the hospital declared him well enough to leave the hospital for relocating to his house in Pretoria.

Siboniso's friends carried him into the home where he and Makeda had been so happy, but as the days went by, he struggled to cope with those happy memories. Soon, he refused to come out of the bedroom.

Makeda, Mozes, and Frank were very worried and disappointed as they had tried their utmost to make his return as comfortable as possible. Siboniso did not even look at the top-of-the-range wheelchair with a computer for writing and drawing, which Frank had attached and programmed.

While they had still been in Cape Town, at the hospital, Makeda had engaged contractors to make the house in Pretoria wheelchair-friendly. There was nothing wrong with Siboniso's arms and torso, so she had wanted to ensure that he would be able to be reasonably independent. Sib was not interested, and he didn't notice the changes in the house. Finally, in desperation, Makeda called a counsellor. Between the two of them, they helped him discover that he needed to accept his limitations and focus on all the things he could still do and learn to do. That was the real beginning of Siboniso's recovery.

⸻ ✦ ⸻

Having started primary school, Bheki insisted on entering the bedroom after school to be with his daddy. He patiently sat with him, made him laugh with school stories, and engaged him in his little boy games.

As always, Makeda was a rock of support, encouraging him to move into his wheelchair, explore the house and experiment with the computer.

In the meeting room in their home was a plain wall where he could project pictures, maps, and statistics. When Sib learned to use a program where the typed words would appear on the wall, he started believing that he could still play an essential role in their organisation. He would ride his wheelchair to the office/meeting room for team discussions and use this new way of communicating. By now, Makeda had become a vital part of the team. Living in Pretoria was an advantage because officials from other African countries often visited the capital of South Africa, where their embassies were located. Among them were delegates of the AU, including many of the contacts Siboniso had made on his travels.

A number of them came to call at their house, first to express their well-wishes for Sib's recovery and condolences for the loss of Imari, who had been well known in the mining industries of Africa. Increasingly though, they visited to express their support for the cause of unity.

In the early stages of recovery, Siboniso wasn't always well enough, mentally or physically, to see anybody. Makeda then represented the team with or without Mozes. Their financial wiz kept himself busy trying to find new sponsors or attending to other financial duties. He also succeeded in selling the mine Imari had managed so well for a good profit. The team agreed to send one quarter of that money to Imari's ageing parents.

Without Mozes, the team would have no income. Frank had quit his position with the US government on becoming a full team member. He rented a place nearby Sib and Makeda, which he used as his office and residence while starting his own IT business.

Frank had volunteered his computer expertise at the headquarters of the AU in Addis Ababa and needed to stay there often, but he always returned for team meetings. While in Ethiopia, he used every opportunity to promote their team's vision of Africa's future. It was a valuable contribution to their cause.

Consequently, Makeda often represented the team when Siboniso wasn't well. Afterwards, she consistently reported to Sib, who was impressed with how she handled discussions with AU delegates. He often had to admit that he would not have considered approaching a problem from her angle, but it was perfect!

Chapter Twenty-Three

IN THE PAST, SIBONISO HAD never been interested in politics and always tried to avoid the subject. He now acknowledged that they needed to know about politics to achieve anything.

Not able or willing to leave the house, he used his time and computer to study the African continent's history and the politics of different countries. He re-read all of Mandela's speeches. His knowledge and understanding of his people deepened. Still, he often despaired because he could not yet see how they would ever succeed in unifying a continent so different in leadership and so preoccupied with fighting on many fronts.

There were battles with insurgents from a neighbouring country or civil unrest in their own country, fighting because of religion, territory claims, or just because of hunger.

———— + ————

Siboniso needed several meetings with the team to find his optimism again. They reminded him that the United States of America had had to go through a terrible civil war before reaching any unity after many years. And what about the European Union? The EU had only started with a few countries agreeing to set shared rules of engagement. After the two world wars, they had to deal with a lot of mistrust, but they still grew into a powerful block, which took decades.

They discussed how the United Nations had started with only five countries. Yet, they had developed into a massive organisation, even if they were always hampered in their efforts for peace by one or more of the original five holding veto power. So, for Africa, they agreed to aim for a federation that would use the best ideas from all three organisations.

The team needed to be included in the South African delegation to gain more influence in the AU. Frank, already well known in the South African government offices because of his computer and internet services, applied for and gained South African nationality. The team's reputation had grown over the years, and they were accepted as a permanent part of the South African delegation to the AU.

— ✦ —

Many years later, a majority of delegates supported a future change into a new federation with a president or a chairperson chosen by the heads of governments for a 5-year term to support stability in leadership. However, it took many more years to establish agreements between states about borders, armies, industries, and how to regulate trade between African states and, as a block, with overseas countries.

Further, they discussed the cost of infrastructure to connect all countries and how to encourage development in poorer countries. One of the most critical agreements was about the finances of a peacekeeping force and its powers to enforce peace between warring parties. Peace would be a prerequisite for all other developments.

— ✦ —

During the 2030 Assembly of the AU, the member states decided to take the leap and establish the UAS—the Union of African States with a two-thirds majority vote. All countries were prepared for this meeting and had the opportunity to nominate their choice for chairperson. The assembly would vote for all new positions after the midday break.

Siboniso was invited to address the assembly in the morning in recognition of his team's success in reaching this momentous result.

Frank had organised for Sib to hold his speech with the computer projecting the words on the big screen for everyone to read. There was total silence as everybody concentrated on reading. Siboniso started by thanking the original members of his team for joining his dream and helping to achieve it. He expressed his deep sadness about losing Imari, pointing out his success in gaining support from the mining industry. He recalled visiting several African states with Nelson Mandela and, later on, by himself. Then, he proudly introduced his wife, Makeda, as the last person to join the team. He explained how she had taken over much of his work because he had dropped out physically and mentally for a while.

Siboniso further expressed his confidence (on-screen) that many delegates who visited their home in Pretoria would no doubt agree that Makeda was an expert in their continent's history and achievements. A further boon was that she was fluent in so many languages.

—— + ——

In the years since, on the committees she joined and in the

meetings that she attended, Makeda had shown how deep her understanding was of the critical national and international issues the UAS would soon face.

Siboniso ended his speech by stating, "That is why the South African delegation will nominate Makeda for the position of the first chairperson of the UAS."

The outgoing president of the AU expressed his thanks and admiration for Siboniso and led the assembly with a standing applause. When it was time to vote for the new positions, they voted overwhelmingly for Makeda as chairperson. She received enthusiastic applause and accepted the invitation to speak.

"The horrific terrorist attack that robbed my dear husband of his ability to speak and walk did not succeed in diminishing our dream of a united Africa. As we got to know most of you, you got to know me and my inspirational teacher, not forgetting the rest of our team: Frank, Mozes and the sorely missed Imari. The UAS will show the world what Africa can do. Thank you for putting your trust in me." Again, applause resounded through the room.

"We, the so-called third-world countries, will show the world that we can achieve better conditions for our people in every country. We will, but only if we all work together and put our collective shoulders under this enormous task."

Makeda took a breath and continued in a determined voice that was inspiring. "It will take hard work, sacrifices, and discipline, but we can do it! The priorities are:

1. A peacekeeping force, currently the African Blue Helmets, consisting of soldiers from all African countries, paid for by their country of origin and trained by officers of the UN Blue Helmets. It will all cost money but will be shared among the member states. It will cost less than most of you spend on your defence portfolio. We can only achieve our goals if we have peace.

2. Improvement of the infrastructure that connects countries and communities. People need access to education and trade routes.

3. Building and staffing medical facilities, schools, trade colleges, and universities. We need teachers, carpenters, electricians, engineers, and more.

4. We need to establish a coordinating facility to support, collect, and distribute the food we grow so that there will be no more hunger."

Makeda took a deep breath and continued with fervour. "Don't be impatient. Let's be partners in this! It will all take time, but Africa can thrive within a decade if we work hard. Keep dreaming. Imagine, in time, that we will design our cars and aeroplanes, build computers, export technology, and other great things.

"Think about the immense Sahara Desert. There is reasonably good soil under the sand. We need to find ways to irrigate the land and make it the food bowl of Africa, maybe by desalinating water from the ocean. Climate change is here to stay and will increase, so we must find creative solutions.

"I want to finish by expressing the hope that no disputes or grudges between members linger. If they do, let's deal with them as Mandela did and unite as one people, where your colour and religion do not matter. Thank you." The applause took a minute and a half.

The End

www.ingramcontent.com/pod-product-compliance
Lightning Source LLC
Chambersburg PA
CBHW061124100726
47911CB00013B/678